Sprouts

of Love

Sprouts

of Love

VALERIE COMER

Acknowledgments

I'm so thankful for my fellow Arcadia Valley Romance authors: Mary Jane Hathaway, Elizabeth Maddrey, Lee Tobin McClain, Danica Favorite, and Annalisa Daughety. If you haven't been following the multi-author series thus far, you really need to jump in and check out all the books!

A special shout-out to Elizabeth Maddrey, who gave me a listening ear and bounced story ideas with me when Evelyn, Ben, and Maisie were a tad uncooperative with story direction. Yes, it happens!

I can't say enough good things about my friend and editor, Nicole, who's been with me since before the beginning of my publishing career. Her keen eye and apt comments are so appreciated.

Thanks to my husband, Jim, who chauffeured me on a road trip to the Twin Falls, Idaho, area in October, 2016, waited patiently while I took nearly a thousand reference photos, and offered his insights of our experiences. I love you, sweetheart. It's you who keeps my love for romance alive.

Thanks to my kids, their spouses, and my grandgirls for their support and interest in my many projects. Special thanks to my daughter who's the cover designer for the entire Arcadia Valley Romance series. It's been fun sharing her expertise with my fellow authors.

I'm always thankful for my fellow inspirational romance author friends at Inspy Romance and my Christian Indie Authors group. I appreciate all who walk the journey with me both personally and professionally.

Thanks to my many readers and fans who've made their home in Arcadia Valley

"It is for this reason that I bow my knees before the Father, after whom all families in heaven above and on earth below receive their names, and pray:

"Father, out of Your honorable and glorious riches, strengthen Your people. Fill their souls with the power of Your Spirit so that through faith the Anointed One will reside in their hearts. **May love be the rich soil where their lives take root.** May it be the bedrock where their lives are founded so that together with all of Your people they will have the power to understand that the love of the Anointed is infinitely long, wide, high, and deep, surpassing everything anyone previously experienced. God, may Your fullness flood their entire beings." (Ephesians 3:14-19 The Voice)

Thank You, Jesus, my Redeemer.

Books by Valerie Comer

Arcadia Valley Romance Novels

Romance Grows in Arcadia Valley
Sprouts of Love

Rooted in Love
Harvest of Love

Farm Fresh Romance Novels

Raspberries and Vinegar
Wild Mint Tea
Sweetened with Honey
Dandelions for Dinner
Plum Upside Down
Berry on Top

Riverbend Romance Novellas

Secretly Yours
Pinky Promise
Sweet Serenade
Team Bride
Merry Kisses

Urban Farm Fresh Romance Novels

Promise of Peppermint
Secrets of Sunbeams
Butterflies on Breezes
Memories of Mist
Wishes on Wildflowers

Christmas in Montana Romances

More Than a Tiara
Other Than a Halo
Better Than a Crown

Chapter 1

*"Y*OU'RE EVELYN FELTON?"

Whatever *that* was all about. The man blocking the entrance to Corinna's Cupboard couldn't be a minute over twenty-five, but that didn't stop him from acting like he owned the place. Eyebrows raised, he assessed her from steely blue eyes.

What had she ever done to him? Nothing. She'd never seen him before... had she? Evelyn stiffened her back and kept the smile in place. "Yes, I'm Evelyn, and I'm here to meet with Ben Kujak about donating garden-grown produce. Is he in?"

Silence reigned for several heartbeats.

Had she asked such a difficult question? The building this charity operated just north of Arcadia Valley's Main Street wasn't that big. If Mr. Kujak wasn't stocking shelves or applying for grants, he likely wasn't on the premises.

The upstart chewed his lip then nodded, stepping aside.

"With a name like Evelyn, I was expecting someone older."

He had to be kidding. Her name wasn't Matilda or Ethel. Evelyn tightened her grip on her messenger bag and raised her eyebrows. "I'm not sure what that's supposed to mean. You haven't answered my question. Is Mr. Kujak available? If not, when's a good time to meet him?"

Muscles rippled the length of his arm as he stretched out his hand. "I'm Ben. Come on in."

"I, um..." She blinked and shook his hand briskly. "Hi." Nobody had told her the man who'd worked miracles starting a charity from nothing was little more than a kid. Scratch that. Definitely not a child, not with how attractive he looked in those cargo shorts and gray T-shirt. Not with his light-brown hair matching the stubble that graced his cheeks and chin.

Evelyn shook her head and took a deep breath. "Like you, I thought I was meeting with someone older."

She'd counted on it, actually. Not that she was easily distracted by good-looking men close to her age, but there was something secure about working with someone older. Somebody who was a husband, a father, maybe even a grandfather. Someone who could guide her as she took on the management of her daughter's resourceful project of using the Akers Garden Center's former greenhouses to grow food for the needy.

Evelyn had no idea what she was doing. She'd truly hoped the recipient of their hard work could smooth the transition. Instead she was stuck with Mr. Do-Good, Junior.

Ben's face morphed into a half-smile. "Well, now that we've gotten all that out of the way, come on into my office." He led the way through a space with tall, sturdy shelving containing a smattering of canned and packaged goods.

How many times had she clutched little Maisie by the hand and searched shelves like these for something besides boxed macaroni and cheese and over-sweetened cereals? Clouds of uncertainty and desperation had permeated their entire life back in Memphis. They hadn't completely dissipated even with Idaho's fresh air and blue summer sky.

Evelyn followed him past another storage room and into a small office. She stopped in the doorway as though she'd rammed into a glass wall. Bricks shored up one corner of a chipped pressboard desk. It was impossible to discern what type of wood it was pretending to be between all of the folders and papers at awkward angles, threatening to slide. Her gaze followed the likely avalanche path to the concrete floor where a few papers and a Styrofoam cup lay beside a full trash can.

Her fingers itched to toss the cup, haul out the garbage, and file this man's papers. How could he get a stitch of work done in a disaster like this?

Ben pointed at an orange plastic chair. "Have a seat." He rounded the desk, scooped together the loose papers in the work area, and deposited them on top of the tallest stack of folders before pulling out his own chair. "Now, what exactly do you want from me?"

Ask not what your food pantry can do for you...

Evelyn perched on the edge of the orange chair and clutched her messenger bag to her chest. "I'm not sure where to start." Why couldn't she remember the speech she'd rehearsed?

He glanced at the clock above the window.

Man, he didn't need to be rude. She took a deep breath. "I'm not sure if you're aware, but elderly Mr. Akers set up a living trust in conjunction with Grace Fellowship. The property in question used to belong to Akers Garden Center and contains an old house, two greenhouses, and numerous garden beds. Volunteers have been growing vegetables there since June, and the first pickings of peas and greens will be ready to harvest in about a week."

"I'm sorry, but I'm not certain what this has to do with me." Ben leaned back in his chair.

Evelyn flinched as it creaked.

Hadn't she just told him? "The volunteers are growing produce for Corinna's Cupboard. We understand that you feed hot meals three evenings a week, and we think that's fantastic. We want to help supply ingredients."

"Uh... that's great. What format exactly are these vegetables coming in?"

She beamed at him. "Garden fresh." He could smile and say thanks anytime.

The man closed his eyes and pinched the bridge of his nose.

Evelyn frowned. "They're organic. Fresh. Full of flavor and nutrients." Why did she feel the need to sell the guy on garden-grown veggies? Didn't he care about the needs of the people for whom he supplied food? Didn't he realize how much money this would save the charity?

Ben took a deep breath and looked across the disastrous desk at her. "Look, Ms. Felton, that sounds wonderful."

She smiled.

"But I'm one man. I don't have time to prepare meals for

forty people from scratch. I have a basic menu I rotate through every two weeks, and that's all I can do."

One man? One guy who was most definitely under thirty did this all by himself? "I-I don't understand."

"There's nothing to understand. I'm not a superhero. I'm one normal guy who happens to run this place single-handedly, and I don't have time to cook from raw ingredients. Thanks for thinking of Corinna's Cupboard, but you'll need to find another outlet for your vegetables." Ben rose. "Was there anything else? Because I have something I need to be doing."

Like clean his office? Evelyn stood. "But..."

"I'm sorry, Evelyn. I really am." He gestured toward the door. "I'd need to be at least three people to handle what you're offering, and I'm not."

Ben couldn't get the memory of the morning's meeting with Evelyn Felton out of his mind. What a contrast she'd been to the needy people who frequented Corinna's Cupboard. She was so vibrant. So full of confidence. So pretty.

So much like Corinna had been.

About that. Extra work aside, he didn't need to notice a woman. He liked donors who sent checks in the mail, hit the PayPal button on the charity's website, or donated to one of the many fundraisers his former in-laws held across the country. Also acceptable: having cases of canned or packaged goods delivered by the local freight company.

Meeting donors face to face only took time he couldn't afford out of his schedule.

Ben drove his hands through his hair. Enough with Evelyn. What had he been doing when she arrived? Counting size-10 cans of peas on the shelf. Hadn't been that hard to count all the way to two.

He and Corinna had bought that acreage with the creek running through it shortly after their wedding with help from her parents. She'd put in a garden amidst the volcanic outcroppings on the property. They'd sat on the back porch, shelling peas into a large bowl and eating them just as quickly, popping the rounded end of the pods and sliding their thumbs down the interior to dislodge the little green orbs. Happy memories of a happier time.

He glared at the huge cans of peas on the shelf. They hailed from a different planet, but he'd told Evelyn the truth. He didn't have time for that much food prep.

All of the shelves were rather bare, but that wasn't unusual. God always provided what Ben needed when he needed it.

Was God trying to provide him with fresh peas? Sweet, succulent peas?

He snorted a laugh as he made his way back to the dismal office. God had better supply an army of volunteers while He was at it.

Ben stopped in the doorway. What had Evelyn seen? His stomach curdled. A full-on disaster. How had it gotten this way? The fourth-hand file cabinet had given up and all but collapsed. He'd removed the files and dumped them on any flat surface. The cabinet was unsalvageable, but he hadn't yet bothered to haul it to the curb on trash day.

He'd gotten in such a rut. Why not just go buy a new file cabinet? He might not want to ask his in-laws for money for that, but he could buy it himself. He could forego riding Halim this afternoon and drive into Twin Falls. It wasn't a hot meal day, and the regulars had already come in to pick up day-old bread and glean from the shelves. He could lock up early.

If Corinna could see him now — see the food cupboard that bore her name — what would she think? Would she be glad he was making a difference, or would she chastise him for the mess it was all in?

He could see the glimmer in Evelyn's narrowed eyes when she looked at his towering paperwork, and he'd spent under fifteen minutes in her presence.

A file cabinet. It was a good place to start. He strode toward the door, fingering the keys in his shorts' pocket.

What if... what if there was something to Evelyn's offer?

Her brown hair, artfully messy, had flowed halfway down her back. Corinna's had been shorter. Black. Evelyn's eyes flashed amber in her eagerness then faded to brown when he'd squashed her hopes. He'd teased Corinna that gazing into her eyes was like drowning in pure coffee.

Why was he even comparing the two women? Corinna was gone, and Evelyn wasn't offering herself as a replacement. No. She offered vegetables. He needed vegetables. Ben's mouth watered. He really liked them fresh from the garden, personally.

He locked up the building. It was just as ugly as the others on this block. Red brick like most of the older storefronts, scuffed and watermarked with age, it crowded the chipped sidewalk. Main Street had been revitalized in the past few years, pulling residents back to shopping locally. A block off Main? Still stuck a hundred years in the past, Corinna's Cupboard shared a block with a tattoo parlor, a couple of bars, a thrift store, and several boarded-up buildings.

Without making a conscious choice, he drove the few blocks out of his way to pass the old Akers' greenhouses. His eyes widened as he rounded the end of the block and saw a row of garden beds overflowing with lush greenery. Several people worked among them.

The truck coasted to a stop at the curb. Ben slid out and walked around to stand on the sidewalk.

Looked like folks were staking and pruning tomatoes. A kid of about ten knelt by the bed nearest him, plucking tufts of green. She glanced over at him.

"Hi." Ben lifted a hand in greeting, his gaze shifting back to the amazing lush scene in front of him. This was what Evelyn had been talking about? Wow.

"Want to help?" the girl asked. "There's lots to do."

Ben turned back to her. What would happen if he played dumb? "I haven't been down this street for a while. What's going on?"

The girl stood and stripped off the dirt-smeared gloves she'd been wearing. Her dark blond hair stuck out of the ponytail trying to corral it. "This is a project from that church over there." She thumbed toward the brick building housing Grace Fellowship a couple of blocks closer to downtown. "The old man wrote a living... a living something. He wanted us to use this place for something that would help people."

Ben searched his earlier conversation for the right words. "Living trust?"

"That's it," she said, snapping her fingers. "I'm Maisie. Who're you? Want to sign up? Cameron's over there. He can help you."

"I'm, uh, Ben." His name wouldn't mean anything to her. "I'm kind of busy these days, so I probably won't volunteer for anything. Thanks, though."

Maisie shoved her hands into the pockets of her shorts. "Everyone's busy." She tilted her head to look up at him. "Did you know that there's lots of people in Arcadia Valley who don't have enough food? Maybe even hundreds."

Why did a kid her age know that or even care? *Play along, Ben.* "Really? Right here?"

"Some of them don't have jobs. And some of them are drunks." She pursed her lips. "There's all kinds of reasons."

"I've noticed a man sitting on the sidewalk holding out a hat."

"That's probably Fred. The doctors had to cut off his leg because of diabetes and he couldn't work anymore."

Ben narrowed his gaze at this child who was barely taller than his waist. "Yes, that's him. Do you know him?"

"I talk to him sometimes. But I usually don't have anything to give him because the old woman by the park is always hungry. I feel bad if I don't give her half my sandwich."

"Rona?" the name slipped out before Ben could censure it.

Maisie tipped her head and gave him a closer look. "Yeah. Rona. You know her? Nobody knows her."

Was he going to tell this child who he was? That he worked to better the lives of people like Fred and Rona? People most others ignored or jeered? He opened his mouth to confess all but, for some reason, reluctance halted his words.

No, he had too much to think about to get embroiled in whatever this kid knew. Whatever this project was for. If they wanted to give him fresh food, couldn't they have thought of the fact they should give him volunteers as well?

Maisie asked him to join the work here. He bit back a sardonic laugh. He should ask her to volunteer for him... but he wouldn't, because she might agree. Might show him up. Anyway, a soup kitchen was no place for a kid.

Ben nodded sagely and offered a smile for the girl. "Thanks for telling me about them. It's nice to find people who care." He turned toward his truck. "Have a great evening."

"If you care about them, you should help us grow food for them."

Ben clamped down on his jaw and didn't turn back. Little did she know.

Chapter 2

S O WHAT DO WE DO NOW?" Evelyn raised the cup of tea and took a sip. It had cooled while she told her tale to her friend. "I know you're not still in charge of the project, but you know more about it than anyone else."

"Hmm. Want a reheat?" Joanna Kraus picked up her sapphire-toned teapot from the crowded tiny counter where it had been dwarfed by a massive floral bouquet. Perks of being engaged to a guy whose family owned a garden center and florist shop.

"Sure."

Joanna topped off both cups and sank onto her seat around the corner of the tiny table. "I must say, I didn't see that twist coming."

Evelyn shook her head and swirled in some honey. She hadn't seen Ben Kujak coming, either. Yes, she'd found his name and contact info on the website, but that was no indication he was young and alone.

The Lord God said, "It is not good for the man to be alone. I will make a helper suitable for him."

Uh, that's not the kind of alone *I meant, God. Thanks, anyway.*

Not that Ben didn't need a helper. What he likely didn't need was a wife. Just like she didn't need a husband. She and Maisie were finally standing on their own and making a go of it. This wasn't the time for complications.

"We do have a lot of volunteers for the greenhouse and gardens," Joanna went on. "I wonder if we could channel some of those over to working at the shelter."

"He did say he'd have to be three or four people to make use of the produce. Do you think he was exaggerating?"

Her friend shook her head. "It's hard to know without seeing it in action. I guess it makes sense we should have checked with him before we started planting, but who'd have thought he'd turn food away?"

"Exactly."

"What did Maisie say?"

Evelyn took a sip of tea. "I didn't tell her. I couldn't bear to break her heart."

"I don't think it will have that effect." Joanna giggled. "She's a bull terrier, that one."

"Too true. Now that you mention it, I can just see her rounding up half a dozen sixth graders to help Ben cook. He wouldn't know what hit him."

"That's not a bad idea."

Evelyn's cup stopped halfway to her mouth. "You're not serious."

"With adult supervision, of course."

Tea sloshed into the saucer from the force as Evelyn set the cup down. "I don't think so."

Joanna tipped her head. "Did you already suggest that, and he shot it down?"

"No." It did seem a reasonable idea. Oh, not the kids' part so much, but trying to get him some help. Had he really asked for volunteers? Evelyn shook her head.

"You're looking lost in thought. There must be more to the story than you're telling me."

Oh, a whole lot more. She hadn't mentioned the piercing brown eyes, the lopsided grin, the hair that begged to be smoothed down. She hadn't mentioned the muscles rippling beneath that T-shirt, either.

Joanna's eyebrows rose. "You said he was younger than you expected. How much younger, exactly?"

"Uh... He's twenty-something. Thirty, tops."

"Cute?"

"That doesn't have anything to do with it. We're talking about his charity here."

"So. Cute."

"A lot of men are cute. Grady, for instance. That doesn't mean I'm trying to steal him away from you."

"Grady is oh, so taken." Joanna beamed and held up her left hand, her diamond solitaire gleaming in the light.

"My point exactly. Just because a man is easy on the eyes doesn't mean a woman has to fall for his charms."

"Oooh, now Ben is charming?"

Evelyn leveled a glare at her friend. "I did not say that. You are reading way too much into this. Overworked is what he is." He really hadn't been all that charming. He'd been blunt and all but pushed her out of his office. How on earth could he work in that mess? Her fingers still itched to file all those papers.

"Okay, I won't push. Although I do think you should open your heart and mind to the possibility. Not Ben, necessarily." Joanna's eyes twinkled as she grinned. "There's always Cameron. I must say I wouldn't mind having you for a sister-in-law."

That would definitely be a benefit of marrying Joanna's brother. Maybe the only one. "I don't think I'm cut out to be the mother of twins. They are certainly a handful." Cameron's wife had walked out on him and their boys a couple of years earlier. The duo, now six, had never met a trouble they couldn't get into, but they *were* awfully cute. Plus they adored Maisie.

"No kidding. Cameron is looking for an after-school program for them come fall. He's probably told you how much juggling we're both doing over the summer. He's taken some vacation time and found a teen to watch them half days. The rest of the time they are all mine, and I'm not getting a lot done on the consulting projects I've got lined up."

Evelyn laughed. "That's not a good enough reason for me to date him. Besides, working for the church coordinating the living trust is my third part-time job, and I've got Maisie to consider, too."

"I know. It's not like Cameron can't afford to pay someone. It's just hard to find dependable help."

Another perk of dating a man like Cameron was that he had a good job, even if it was with Stargil. Too bad they were a commercial food processing plant. Cameron's family wouldn't lack the necessities of life, while Evelyn and her daughter had gone without more times than she could count.

He would certainly be a more stable choice than someone like Ben Kujak. Was Ben even able to draw a salary from the charity?

And why, exactly, was she even thinking about dating or marrying? Here she was, finally making ends meet for Maisie and her. She didn't need a man to simplify — or complicate — their lives.

"...after-school program?"

Evelyn blinked her friend's face back into focus. "Pardon me?"

"I asked if there was any news on the after-school program at the greenhouse. You know, through the living trust."

"Oh." Evelyn sighed. "Who knew there would be so much red tape in setting everything up? There's no hope of getting things running for this fall. I guess it was an overly ambitious idea considering all the government hoops. And, of course, we can't advertise for staff until we have approval, and the hiring process won't happen overnight, either."

"So... a January launch, then?"

Evelyn shook her head. "The house on the property needs some upgrades. We've got a contractor coming in later this fall to get started. Drew Harrison. I think we're better off focusing on a grand opening next August when school goes back in. Any sooner, and we're rushing it."

Joanna sighed. "I'll let Cameron know he's on his own for another year. For his sake, I was hoping the program would be in place before my wedding."

"You've set a date?"

"First Saturday of June. When one's fiancé manages a

garden center, there isn't really a good time of year. I was hoping for earlier, but my parents are in England and can't make it sooner."

Not something Evelyn would have to consider when — or rather, if — she ever planned a wedding. Her parents had washed their hands of her when she got pregnant with Maisie. She doubted she'd even bother to let them know. Not that marriage was on the table, so it wasn't going to be an issue one way or the other.

Evelyn smiled at Joanna. "I'm so happy for you both." She really was. "Okay, back to the Grace Greenhouse project. Any ideas of somewhere else we can get rid of all that produce? Should we try for a booth at the farmers market?"

"That might be an idea. I hate to give up on the primary purpose, though."

"We could donate the proceeds, though that means the homeless people will miss out on all the fresh food." Or was it just that she wanted an excuse to see Ben Kujak again? She wouldn't admit that to Joanna in a million years.

"I beat you three games straight, man." Felipe Espinoza tossed the controller onto Ben's coffee table. "I like this trend."

Ben leaned back in his chair. "Sorry. My head's not in it today."

"No need to be sorry. I like winning for a change." Felipe stood and stretched from side to side. "Got any pop in your fridge? Because I doubt you have anything stronger."

"There's pop. Help yourself." He'd become a teetotaler after the accident, and Felipe knew it. "Grab some chips while you're at it."

Felipe ambled into the kitchen. A cupboard door opened and a bag rustled. "Got any dip?"

"Yeah, in the fridge. Picked up an eggplant dip at the farmers market last Saturday. Pretty good."

"Eggplant?" The fridge door opened. "Don't you have anything normal?"

Ben closed his eyes. "Don't knock it 'til you've tried it."

A few minutes later Felipe plunked an armload of snacks onto the coffee table. "I don't understand you, man." He tore the bag of chips open and dunked one into the dip. "You're too good for the potato chips Stargil makes right here in town. You need artisan chips. Artisan dip. And yet at the soup kitchen you're all about the industrial canned food. What gives?" He popped the chip in his mouth.

"Do you know how much this stuff costs? The foundation isn't made of money." Although it was a long way from empty and paid him a decent salary. "I feed forty people three nights a week. They don't care, so long as it is tasty and filling."

Felipe grimaced and peered at the jar's label. "What is in this stuff? You're right, the homeless people don't want it. *I* don't want it. Are you sure there's nothing else?"

"You want different snacks, you bring them next time."

"I think I will." Felipe screwed the lid back on the dip, opened the can of pop, and grabbed a handful of chips. "So, what's got you distracted tonight?"

"Food, if you must know."

Felipe barked out a laugh then took a closer look. "You're serious?"

Okay, so it wasn't just food. It was Evelyn Felton's visit to Corinna's Cupboard two days ago. He hadn't been able to get his head in the game since, even though he'd fixed a roast beef dinner for forty in the interim, complete with mashed potatoes, gravy, and the second to last can of peas. The beef and potatoes hadn't been too bad, but the peas had rolled around in his gut like so many olive-green marbles. Disgusting in color, texture, and flavor.

And to think he'd turned down fresh ones.

"What is it about food that makes you so melancholy, my friend? Getting tired of your own cooking? You have a standing invitation to our house, you know. Mexican at its finest."

"I've always been tired of my own cooking. That's nothing new." Just as the light had gone out of his life when Corinna died, so had all the flavors turned to cardboard. Maybe it was a positive sign he was finally noticing.

A man didn't get twenty years on the police force, even in a small town, without paying attention. Ben felt the scrutiny as Felipe seemed to weigh the evidence with what he saw on Ben's face. "Okay, so it's not the preparation of food. Perhaps it is the paradox of sharing a table with several dozen needy people yet sitting alone in your kitchen."

Ben surged to his feet and angled a look out the window. Halim, Penny, and Rapunzel stood in the shade of a big elm. Two horses and a pony, representing the family Ben had once had. "A woman came into the soup kitchen the other day."

"Ah. A woman."

Ben rolled his eyes. Not that Felipe could see from behind him. "She offered fresh garden produce to the Cupboard."

"That's terrific! What a big help that will be to stretch the dollars."

"You do realize what fresh vegetables look like?" Ben turned to face his friend. "Dirt, peels, and all that?"

"I have met a vegetable or two in my day, yes. This is a problem how?"

"I'm one guy, Felipe. I'm already there nearly forty hours a week. I don't have time to prepare vegetables from scratch as well as everything else I'm doing." He thumbed over his shoulder. "See those horses? They haven't been ridden in over a week."

"I would offer to ride with you, but I am working the next four days. Someone has to make sure the coffee and doughnuts in this town don't go to waste."

"That would be criminal."

"Of course, there's always the chance I might get to write a traffic violation ticket."

Felipe might make light of his job, but Ben knew all too well he took it seriously on duty.

Black night. Red and blue strobe lights. Sirens.

Ben scrubbed at his face. If only the memories wouldn't attack without notice. To be fair, the actual nightmares had faded over time. The pain of losing Corinna and Zoey wasn't as sharp as it had been, thank the Lord, but the gash remained, as deep and wide as the Snake River Canyon and nearly as long.

"So about this woman who offered you vegetables." His friend's voice was gentle. "Young? Old?"

"No one can take Corinna's place, Felipe. No one."

"Five years, my friend. You deserve to be happy again."

"I'm not sure that I do. Does anyone deserve happiness?"

"Does anyone deserve to be alone and miserable?"

Ben dropped back into his chair. "Great, now I'm miserable."

"There's more to life than work. Than running a charity as a tribute to your late wife." Felipe leaned closer. "She's gone, Ben. You told me she didn't want you to mourn her for the rest of your life."

He didn't want to remember, yet he couldn't forget the last words she'd said before the light dimmed in her eyes.

Chapter 3

THE FARMERS MARKET BUSTLED with activity as Evelyn and Maisie approached the wide-open doors. Most small towns had an outdoor market, but not Arcadia Valley. The original owner had built this building as large as an arena. Music trickled out amid the babble of voices and laughter. Aromas rode on the waves of the cacophony.

"Can we get a corn dog, Mom?"

"Maybe." Certainly better than the usual canine Maisie begged for. Or whatever the most recent animal had been. Evelyn was so used to saying no to the barrage that all the begging blended. "First we need to find the manager."

Evelyn's eyes adjusted from the brilliant sunshine, and her heart sank as she took in the melee. She should've left a message when the manager didn't answer her phone yesterday instead of deciding to pop in. Evelyn set her hands on Maisie's shoulders and steered her daughter into the thick of the crowd toward the central office, past booths overflowing with handmade aprons, kettle corn, produce, dog treats... the variety was dizzying. The Friends of the

Library even hosted a bake sale. Not a single booth was vacant as far as she could see.

But that was just today, right? Surely the library didn't attend every week, so that spot might be open next Saturday.

Evelyn reached past Maisie and tapped on the open office door. The command center sat slightly above the market floor with windows all around. Empty. What now?

"Mom, Kaleena waved at me." Maisie tugged at her arm. "Can I go with her and see the market? I promise we won't leave."

Maisie's friend hung back from where her mother haggled with a vendor, both women with moving mouths and flailing hands. The younger Espinozas crowded around their mother.

"Constance doesn't need one more kid to watch over."

"We're big enough to see the market alone. We're almost eleven. Not babies."

Evelyn sighed. "If her mom agrees. If not, you get right back over to me, missy." Maybe she was being overprotective because of the crowd. After all, her daughter rode her bike all around town unaccompanied.

Maisie rolled her eyes then dashed down the few steps and disappeared into the throng of humanity. A moment later she popped up beside the Espinozas then waved to Evelyn. She and Kaleena linked arms and sidled away, heads bent together.

Okay. So, where was the manager? The young woman was new this year. Evelyn had seen her a couple of times when she'd shopped here. What was her name? Kelly? Kathy? No, something else.

"Looking for Kate?" asked the young woman at a nearby booth. "She just went out to walk the market and check in with the vendors. She'll probably be back in half an hour or so."

Evelyn's heart sank. It would take at least that long to see everyone. "Yes, I was hoping to catch her. I wanted to ask about renting a stall."

The woman offered a lopsided smile. "I happen to know the answer to that question. We're booked solid for the summer with a waiting list."

"But..."

"I'm sorry. You can see how full we are. What did you want to sell?"

"I'm Evelyn Felton, the manager of the Akers Living Trust. We've got two greenhouses and a yard full of garden beds with produce that will soon be ready for harvest."

"Uh... it's always best to plan ahead."

"I know. Our other outlet fell through." Okay, she hadn't done a good job of planning ahead even there. She'd just assumed... never a good idea. "We're trying to raise money for the soup kitchen. Corinna's Cupboard." Although everything would have been so much easier if Ben had just smiled and said, "thank you, drop the food off at the back door."

"Why not donate it directly? I'm sure Ben can use vegetables as well as money." She let out a half-smile. "I'm Brooke Lockwood, by the way. I've driven by your lot, and it looks like it is thriving. I wondered who was running it."

"It's a joint project between the Akers Garden Center and Grace Fellowship. I'm just the coordinator." Who ought to be fired. "As for donating directly, Ben turned it down. Said he didn't have the volunteers to process raw food."

"Yeah. He runs that place by himself. He's never asked for help that I know of. He's not much for depending on other people."

"Sometimes we don't have a choice." Having been homeless with a small child in tow, Evelyn had had to get over that mentality.

"There's always a choice." Brooke turned to sell three dozen eggs to a client while Evelyn scanned the crowd one more time. "I wish I had better news for you."

"Yeah, me, too."

Brooke stood on tiptoe and craned to look around. "Oh, there she is. Do you see her? She's talking to my sister Riley, the woman with the dog treats." She pointed.

"I think so. I'll see if I can intercept her there." Evelyn smiled at Brooke. "It was nice to meet you. I'll be back for a dozen eggs, unless they are all spoken for?"

"That'd be great. Hurry, though. Kate won't be with Riley for long."

Evelyn angled through the crowd, her gaze so fixed on the doggy banner that she nearly mowed over the woman with the clipboard. "Oh! Sorry. Are you the manager?"

"Yes, I'm Kate Groves. What can I do for you?"

Before Evelyn had managed two sentences, Kate's head was already shaking. "I'm so sorry, but no. I'd love to expand the market to make room for drop-ins, but it sure won't be this summer."

"I saw the Friends of the Library booth. Are they here every week?"

"No, but a different organization is booked each week clear through September. 4-H has it one week. The Rotary. Mothers Against Drunk Driving." Kate shrugged. "That sort of thing. I'm sorry."

"But—" Evelyn clamped off her words. So much for her and Joanna's bright idea to sell here. She was back to square one. "Thanks, anyway." It wasn't Kate's problem. It was one-hundred percent Evelyn's.

Someone tapped Kate on the shoulder and she turned away.

"Mom!" called Maisie from the counter at the dog treat booth.

Uh oh. Evelyn forced a smile and edged nearer.

"How about a kitten?" Maisie's brown eyes sparkled as she cradled a tiny ball of fluff against her chest. "Please, Mom?"

Evelyn closed her eyes with a sigh. "No, Maisie. No kitten."

"I'll clean the litter box. I promise. No one will even know it's there, even you. Please?"

The vendor chuckled. "Every kid needs a pet."

Evelyn shook her head. "Not this one. Thanks, anyway." She plucked the kitten out of Maisie's grasp and handed it to the woman then put her arm around Maisie's shoulder and guided her away. Kaleena trailed behind. "Maisie, no means no. We are *not* getting a pet of any kind, okay? Besides the rules — and there *are* rules I signed to uphold — there's time and money. Please stop asking."

"But Kaleena has a—"

"Maisie."

"Fine, Mom." Maisie's jaw set.

Evelyn steeled herself against the disappointment on her daughter's face. It matched the sinking in her own belly at the thought of having no place to send all those vegetables. What was she going to do now?

Ben squinted at the clock on Sunday morning. Five o'clock? He rolled over and pulled the pillow over his head. Way too early on his day off. He didn't need to be anywhere until church, and he'd skipped often enough in recent months no one would likely notice if he didn't show up today.

The sign in front of Grace Fellowship said services were at eleven. He and Corinna had attended church in Twin Falls, where they'd grown up. But maybe he should try one closer to home. One that apparently cared about the homeless and needy.

Seriously, though. Five o'clock?

Sunshine glowed through the blinds. Gypsy barked. Halim whinnied.

Maybe getting up wouldn't be so terrible. He could ride Halim this morning and take Penny out later. Felipe hadn't had time to ride lately, nor drop one of his kids by to ride Rapunzel. Maybe Ben should board Penny somewhere she could be exercised regularly. Zoey's pony, too.

Wonder if Evelyn rides?

No, he couldn't think that… but hadn't Corinna's last wish been for him to be happy? What did that even mean without her?

33

Ben surged out of bed and yanked on jeans and a T-shirt. He stuffed his feet into a pair of old, scuffed boots and jogged out to the corral. He saddled Halim and gave the gelding his head. The creek gurgled through the gully on its way to join the Snake River. The sun peeked through the scrub pine and warmed his skin. Songbirds chirped and fluttered.

He breathed deeply as he slowed Halim to a trot. He'd been through this before. Round and round. It was getting easier, though. Bit by bit. Zoey would have been seven now, not much younger than that girl at the greenhouse garden. What had her name been? Maisie. Now that was a kid who was focused. She talked like the boss.

Ben chuckled, and Halim's ears twitched. Maybe Maisie *was* the boss. Who knew? But Evelyn was the one who'd come by and talked to him. Had he been too brusque with her? He'd only told the truth, but there might have been a nicer way to put it. She was only trying to help, after all.

Maybe they could work something out.

He wouldn't let his mind dwell on exactly what that might look like.

"We're headed for lunch at the Sunrise. Want to come?" Joanna made puppy dog eyes at Evelyn after church.

"I'm not a date-buster, thanks."

"It's not a date. Cameron and the boys are coming, too."

"Are you trying to set me up with your brother again?"

"Who, me?" Joanna linked her arm through Evelyn's as

the crowd flowed past them into the summer sunshine. "Well, maybe. But I'm not sure I'm up for all the testosterone with four guys for company, even if half of them are only six years old."

Maisie ducked between an older couple and grabbed Evelyn's hand. "Mom, can we get a hamster? Please? Ginny's hamster had babies. She said they're so sweet."

"No, Maisie."

"Hamsters don't run around loose, so it doesn't matter if we live in an apartment. I'll clean the cage. Promise."

"Our building doesn't allow pets." Something Evelyn was thankful for, or she'd have a hard time standing up to her daughter. "Which I believe I've mentioned to you before."

"But I hear a dog sometimes from inside Number Four. And I saw a cat in a window last week."

"Just because other tenants are breaking the agreement doesn't mean we will. The answer is no."

Maisie crossed her arms over her chest and scowled.

"Wow, that's quite a lower lip." Grady came up beside Joanna and slid his arm around her. "Is that because your mom said you're going out for lunch with us?"

Maisie brightened. "Really? We are? Where to?"

Evelyn sighed. Talk about cornered. Beyond Grady, Cameron corralled the twins. Closer to the door, Mr. Marshall shook hands with... Ben Kujak? Since when did he attend Grace Fellowship? She'd have noticed him if he'd been here before. And if he'd been here before, he'd have known about the greenhouse project.

Ben smiled, nodded, and said something to Mr. Marshall. Then his gaze went past the elder's head and collided with hers. The air in the room seemed to buzz and close in on her as though no one else were present. But that was silly.

Evelyn forced a smile and fluttered her hand in a wave.

He gave her a little smile and nod before turning back to Mr. Marshall.

"Who's that?" Joanna wanted to know.

Evelyn shook her head. "Um, Ben Kujak. From Corinna's Cupboard."

"That was a long look he gave you."

It had felt like time stood still, to be honest. Like she'd stepped through some magic portal into a different dimension. That's what she got for reading *The Lion, the Witch, and the Wardrobe* to Maisie before bed. Next she'd be seeing fauns and having tea with beavers.

"I missed something." Grady glanced around. "Who are we talking about here?"

"Just the guy who runs Corinna's Cupboard." Evelyn tightened her arm around Maisie's shoulder. "You said the Sunrise?" She still wasn't rolling in riches, but she could afford an occasional lunch out.

"Oh, is that Ben Kujak? I've been meaning to go down and meet the guy. Just a sec." Grady cut a line across the foyer.

Mr. Marshall clapped Ben on the shoulder and turned away. Ben's eyes found hers again, just before Grady broke the line of vision.

Evelyn felt a slow burn creep up her cheeks. He'd caught her staring, what, three times since church ended? Not good. Not good at all.

Cameron approached, a boy's hand gripped in each of

his. "We ready to go?" His gaze lingered on Evelyn's. "You look nice today."

"Thanks." Why did it feel weird to have Cameron's attention? He was a fine man who was rediscovering his Christian faith. He'd be perfect for her. Sort of perfect.

The group shifted toward the open doors, where summer sunshine — and likely blistering heat — awaited them. Closer to where Grady and Ben stood talking.

"A group of us are going out for lunch," she heard Grady say. "Why don't you join us?"

Joanna's elbow dug into Evelyn's side.

Ben's gaze snagged on Evelyn's one more time. "Sure. Why not?"

Chapter 4

EN FELT LIKE HALIM had knocked him against the corral timbers. He couldn't deny that he'd checked out Grace Fellowship this morning to catch another glimpse of Evelyn and to find out more about her project. He should have realized she was married with kids.

"This is my fiancée, Joanna, and her brother Cameron. These two little hoodlums are his twins, Evan and Oliver." Grady ruffled the hair of the redheaded boy at his side.

Cameron reached out and took Ben's hand with a mighty squeeze that left Ben's fingers slightly numb. Was that some kind of warning? "Pleased to meet you."

The other man didn't sound pleased. "Same."

"This is our friend Evelyn, whom I believe you've already met?"

"I have. Nice to see you again, Evelyn."

Cameron widened his stance, arms crossed over his chest.

Okay, so maybe the two were dating? Grady hadn't introduced them as a couple, and hopefully the guy wouldn't be that insecure if they were married. And Evelyn shouldn't be watching Ben if that were the case.

"Welcome to Grace Fellowship," said Evelyn. "I hope you enjoyed the service this morning."

"I did. Good music and an uplifting sermon. I usually attend Twin Falls Gospel Church but thought I'd try something closer to home this morning."

"Where'd Maisie go?" Grady looked around. "There she is. Hey, Maisie! Come here. We're ready to go, and I want you to meet Ben Kujak."

The child turned away from a gaggle of girls. Her face brightened when she saw Ben. "You're the guy who stopped by the greenhouse! Did you decide you want to volunteer after all?"

Grady laughed. "This is Evelyn's daughter, Maisie. She's our mastermind and energy source. Also, she doesn't take no for an answer." He looked around the group. "So that's eight of us. Want to call the Sunrise and see if they'll push two tables together for us, love?"

"Sure." His fiancée pulled out a sparkling blue phone and turned aside as the rest of the gang trouped out.

Ben hung back. What had he gotten himself into? This was crazy. He'd spent so much time alone or working since the accident he couldn't even remember when he'd last been out with a group of friends. If it hadn't been for Felipe's dogged determination, he'd have been even more isolated.

These weren't really his friends, for all Grady seemed welcoming. At least not yet. And somehow Ben doubted he and Cameron would ever be best buds. Before he walked away, though, he needed to know if Evelyn and Cameron were a couple.

Walked away? Where on earth were his thoughts going? It seemed part of him had decided to pursue Evelyn Felton. She and her daughter — Ben should have realized their relationship; they were cut from the same cloth — strolled down the sidewalk toward downtown, arms around each other.

Ben's breath caught. For an instant, he could see Corinna and Zoey walking like that, but they'd never had the chance. They were gone, but he wasn't.

"Coming, Ben?" Joanna stood beside him. "Or are you having second thoughts?"

"No second thoughts." At least none he'd tell this woman about. He grinned at her. "A man has to have lunch."

"So do we all. I can't wait to hear the details about Corinna's Cupboard and what you're doing there. I've only lived in Arcadia Valley a few months, and wasn't even aware of the homeless problem here until Maisie enlightened me."

Maisie? Why would a kid that age even care? Maybe there was something to Grady's claim that she was the mastermind. She'd sure seemed the boss of the garden beds.

He shook his head as he pulled his truck keys from his pocket. "I'll meet you there."

A few minutes later he entered the café. Grady stood with his hands on the back of a chair at the end of a pair of tables and waved Ben to the seat around the corner from him.

Where would that put Evelyn? She wasn't here yet, though Ben hadn't seen her along the way. She must've taken a shortcut or maybe caught a ride with Cameron after all. He crossed the space and took the appointed seat. "Thank you. They've got a great menu here."

Joanna leaned forward across the table. "We love it because so many of the ingredients are fresh. Their menu shifts by what's available in season."

Her voice faded away as Evelyn entered the café laughing with Cameron, the kids in front of them. Ben's heart sank, but that was ridiculous. He should have expected she was already taken.

Cameron herded his boys around the table to Ben's side and took a seat between them. Evelyn slid in beside Joanna, her daughter next to her.

The big question was, how taken was she?

The really big question was, why did it matter? While he didn't miss Corinna with every fiber of his being as he had for the first two or three years, he hadn't seriously thought about remarriage.

Whoa.

He wasn't considering it now, either. Evelyn had vegetables. He had a soup kitchen. They could work together with no romantic involvement. But since when was he even considering fresh produce as an option? He'd told the truth. There was just him but, while he was devoted to running the charity, he had no intention of spending his days off there as well, prepping veggies.

"Can I get you anything to drink?" The server slid a menu in front of him.

"Coffee, please. Black." He glanced to see if the breakfast options had changed since his last visit, but they hadn't, so he set it back down, closed.

Evelyn met his gaze over her menu, but she quickly looked down, a faint flush brushing her cheeks.

41

Whatever Cameron thought, Evelyn was free. Ben's spirits lifted. That might be a childish reaction to the other man, but he couldn't help it. He'd see what happened.

The others around the table consulted about the menu items and, when the server returned with their drinks a few minutes later, they placed their orders.

"Good choice," Grady said with a laugh. "It's impossible to go wrong with any of the Delis sausages."

"Eggs Benedict with sausage is my favorite thing on the menu. I'd have to come here a whole lot more often than once a month before I'd need to choose something else."

"I hear you, man." Grady leaned back in his chair. "So you're the guy who runs Corinna's Cupboard. How does that work out for you?"

Maisie shushed the twin across the table from her and turned to him expectantly.

Call him chicken, but Ben didn't want to talk about Corinna and Zoey right now. "It operates as a trust, with various monthly donors topping off the base funding put in place by a private foundation."

"I know about trusts," Maisie informed him. "That's what the greenhouse garden has, too."

Joanna looked down the table to the girl. "There are different kinds. His is probably different than ours."

"I answer to a board, who make many of the decisions. But I do all the work." Some days it sure felt like it.

"Mom wouldn't let me come see where you work."

Ben dared a glance at Evelyn. She was looking down at her napkin. "It's not a great neighborhood for kids to be."

Maisie rolled her eyes. "I already told you I'm friends

with Rona. She's not dangerous."

"No, she's not. But there are others who come, too. Some have drug problems, for instance." He didn't even want to consider what some of the regulars would think of this winsome child. He would've kept Zoey far from there, too.

"Mom said you didn't want our vegetables. That's silly."

Wow, this kid didn't mince words. "Only because I don't have time to shell peas and freeze or can them. It would take too many extra hours."

The child shrugged. "Then you ask for help."

Did she think he hadn't tried? Even though Corinna's parents chaired the foundation, they never swung by to roll their sleeves up. No one did. They all seemed content to let him handle everything. He pushed a smile at Maisie. "People are pretty busy already."

Grady chuckled, breaking the one-on-one. "You'd be amazed at the volunteers Maisie can drum up if you turn her loose. How many do we have at the greenhouse now? Fifty?"

The girl nodded. "About that. A few have dropped off since we began in April."

Ben snapped his gaping jaw shut.

"An amazing number of them are adults, too," Grady went on. "This kid is a force to be reckoned with."

"That's great." What else could Ben say? It wasn't like he had a Maisie in his life.

By the tilt of the girl's head, though, he wasn't so sure about that. "How many people do you need to help you?"

"Maisie." Evelyn slid her arm across her daughter's shoulders. "You can't keep taking on things. School will soon be back in."

"Thankfully," muttered Cameron.

"I didn't mean me, Mom. You already said I couldn't go there." Maisie glared at Evelyn. "We can find other people. Grown-ups."

"Maybe." Evelyn glanced his way from under lowered lashes.

"Like you, Mom. You're not working Saturdays, right?"

"She works every other day of the week, Maisie," Joanna interjected. "Leave her with some free time."

Maisie scowled. "Mom could if she wanted to."

The server slid plates of food down the far end of the table to the delight of the twins.

Whew. This was one intense kid. No surprise that adults had trouble refusing her.

Evelyn took another bite of her kale and sausage chowder. She happened to agree with Ben. Any sausage made by Nico Delis was the perfect food.

She might agree with him on other counts, too, but it was hard to know. The conversation swirled around her, but all she really knew was that two men watched her from the other side of the table. Ben kept glancing her way during any lull in the conversation, as though inviting her to take part. Cameron only glowered.

Had she ever really encouraged Joanna's brother? He was a nice enough man, but not for her. Probably there was no Mr. Right. She'd decided long ago to focus on her relationship with Jesus and with her daughter and accept her lot in life. Why was she even having second thoughts?

That was easy. Ben Kujak. It was also ridiculous. He'd all but pushed her out of Corinna's Cupboard that day last week. So why couldn't she get him out of her mind just as easily?

Gah.

Other guests drifted toward the cash register. The wait staff began cleaning around them.

"Guess we should get going." Grady pushed back his chair. "I keep forgetting they close at two."

Evelyn spooned up the last of her soup. A glance at her daughter's plate revealed the grilled ham-and-cheese long gone. Maisie shepherded the twins outside while the adults lingered near the till. Grady paid for his and Joanna's lunches. Evelyn stepped closer, opening her wallet.

"May I?"

Ben's voice was so close to her ear she jumped.

"Thanks, but it's okay. I can get it."

"I'd like to."

She met his gaze. Those warm brown eyes looked back at her. Something passed between them. Who could say what it was? "Thank you."

"I was going to offer," said Cameron.

"I've got it." Ben flashed a smile at the other man. A triumphant one?

Oh, man. What was she going to do? This was crazy. Evelyn fled outside to wait with the children.

"I want a puppy," came Evan's voice.

"Me, too." Maisie stood with her back to Evelyn. "Or even a kitten. But what I really want is a horse."

Evelyn sighed. It never ended.

"Where would you keep it at the apartment?" asked Evan. "Is there a pasture?"

"I like horses, too," put in Oliver. "Daddy said we can go to day camp at Bigby Farm. They have horses."

Maisie's shoulders sagged as the door behind Evelyn opened and closed. "I don't think I can go to day camp. Does it cost money?"

Evan shrugged.

"Horses do, Mom said," Maisie went on. "You have to have pastures and saddles and a whole bunch of stuff. That's why I can't have a horse."

A low chuckle startled Evelyn. "Is that your daughter's secret wish?"

She turned to face Ben. "Not so secret, I'm afraid. She tells anyone who will listen. Even six-year-old boys with no concept of what it entails and no connections to make her dreams come true."

"Dreams come true, huh?" Ben's jaw tightened just a little. "In my experience, most of them don't."

Evelyn stared at him. "But they can. At least some of them." Otherwise she'd still be on the streets of Memphis, trying to keep a little girl fed and safe. "It doesn't hurt to have dreams."

"It hurts when you think they've come true, and they're shattered." He shook his head. "Sorry. Life has thrown me a few curve balls."

He thought he was the only one? Well, she wouldn't enlighten him. Whatever she'd thought she'd seen in him... time to forget it.

Chapter 5

EN DROVE HOME the long way. Why had he said that to Evelyn? He could've made a little girl very happy. A casual, "hey, I have horses. Want to come out for a ride?" and the kid would have been in seventh heaven. Her mother would have been smiling.

Smiling was good.

Scowling was bad.

He did too little of the first and far too much of the second. He'd tucked his life into tidy little compartments, not allowing them to intersect. Not allowing his heart to become engaged. Would it be so bad to let someone in? Someone who could bring life and warmth to the dry places? Yes, it would. Everything he loved turned to ashes. The evidence was right here. He pulled off the highway beside the white cross.

"Be happy. Make a difference." She'd said it to him right here. Her final words.

"Oh, Corinna. I don't know how to be happy without you." The second part was easier. With the help of her parents, he *was* making a difference. Happiness, though... that was something else entirely.

In his mind's eye, she grinned at him, tossing back her short black hair, her dark eyes twinkling with life and laughter. "You're so serious," she teased. "Come on. Have some fun. Let's dance." *Let's play. Let's ride.*

She'd whirled into his life back in high school, when he'd been at the lowest point in his existence — at least, the lowest point until that night five years ago. She'd been all the sunshine and laughter a guy could ever want. He'd been smitten from the first moment, determined to become a better man and reignite his love for God.

Ben stared at the white cross with the wreath of plastic flowers Corinna's mom had draped around it. For the first time, he could stand here and remember the better days.

But letting go? That opened up all sorts of possibilities he wasn't ready for. For a short while after meeting Evelyn, he'd toyed with the idea, but the thought of another little girl riding Zoey's pony, another woman riding Corinna's mare and living in the house he and Corinna had built together... he couldn't do it.

Sure, he was lonely. But when Corinna had said for him to be happy, had she really meant he should love someone else and remarry?

It was safer to guard his heart so he'd never feel this sort of pain again.

"What was all that about?" Joanna bumped Evelyn's arm.

Evelyn shook her head. There was no point in pretending she didn't know what her friend referred to. "I have no idea. He seemed to be having a good time, but then he got all surly and walked away."

"A mystery man."

Yeah. Evelyn could do without theatrics, though. After all those lingering looks, she hadn't expected to be snubbed outside the café. She didn't need his mood swings.

"Not so mysterious." Cameron stood beside his sister. "His wife and kid were killed in a car accident a few years ago. I remember reading about it in the paper. Drunk driver."

"Oh, no. That must have been so hard for him." It did explain a few things.

"Sometimes bad stuff happens, and you need to move on." Cameron held Evelyn's gaze. "It takes time, though."

Was Cameron hinting at something? She'd tried not to encourage him. "It can take time. I get that." How many years was a few?

Grady took Joanna's hand. "See you all later. We're headed out for the day."

"Have fun!" Evelyn didn't want to be alone with Cameron. Where was Maisie?

"Listen, I overheard the kids."

Evelyn glanced up at Cameron. "Oh?" Did she even want to know which part?

He lowered his voice. "About Bigby Farm. They have a great summer camp. Would you mind if I enrolled Maisie for a week or two with the boys? I can pick her up and drop her off."

"No, that's okay."

Cameron's hand rested on her arm. "Why not? You don't have to do everything yourself, Evelyn. It's all right to accept help from a friend."

Were they friends? Did she want to be? Could they be friends without it spilling over into more? "Thanks, Cameron. For Maisie's sake, I'd better say no." She took a step back.

His brow furrowed as his hand dropped away. "But she wants to. That's what she and the twins are talking about. How they're so lucky to go. I can afford to send her, too."

"It's not just the money, Cameron. It's her expectations. I do appreciate the offer, though."

"What do you mean by her expectations?" He lowered his voice, his gaze intent on hers.

Beyond him, the kids chattered away. No one seemed to be listening. "I don't want her to get hurt any more than she has been."

"I don't understand. How will day camp hurt her?"

He was going to make her spell it out. Evelyn sighed. "She'll expect you to keep giving her things. That more will come of it."

Cameron's eyes softened. "You mean me and you?"

"That's part of it. Yes."

"There could be a me and you. We could date. Try it out. See what happens."

Like trying on a pair of shoes at Payless? She could do with a few less raging hormones than when Maisie had been conceived after that high school football game, but surely some attraction would not go amiss. She felt more for Ben Kujak, whom she'd met all of twice, than she did for Cameron Kraus.

She backed up another step. "I think being friends is good. Like we are now."

Hurt flickered across his face. "Friends give each other gifts, too. I'd like to do this for Maisie. For you."

Was she crazy to turn this literal gift horse away? Maybe, but the offer came with too much baggage. She couldn't let herself be indebted to Cameron, even if he promised it was a full-on gift. Even if it would make Maisie's dream come true. "I really appreciate the thought, but I just can't. I hope you'll understand."

"I don't." His hands reached for hers.

Evelyn shook her head and stuffed her hands in her skirt pockets. "Please don't, Cameron."

"I don't see why it's so wrong to give gifts to your friends. I'm thankful for the steady job I have that covers everything the boys and I need."

Was the man completely deaf? Evelyn sidestepped him and tapped Maisie on the shoulder. "Come along, sweetie."

"Can I go to Bigby Farm like Oliver and Evan, Mom? They have horses."

"No, sweetie, you can't." She draped an arm over her daughter's shoulder and steered her down the sidewalk. Any second now Cameron would make his offer loud enough for Maisie to hear, and then what would happen? Evelyn gritted her teeth until they'd turned the corner at the end of the block. Finally she dared breathe.

"What's wrong, Mom?"

Nothing she could explain to a ten-year-old. Evelyn shoved down the unpleasant feelings and hunted for something warm and happy to talk about. All that came up in her mind was Ben. As though that applied to him. He had just as much angst as Cameron. As much as the guys she'd known in high school back in Memphis. Didn't the male species grow up past that? Women sure did, at least ones who'd found themselves with a child to support at a young age.

"Mom?"

Evelyn forced a smile to her face as she looked down at Maisie. "Hey, sweetie. How about we ride our bikes out to the creek and go for a swim this afternoon? Would you like to?"

"That sounds fun. Can I invite a friend?"

She hesitated. Where had the days gone when her daughter was content to simply spend time together? "I suppose so."

"Yay! Can I use your phone to call Kaleena?"

"May I," she corrected automatically, handing over her cell. Why did Maisie have to grow up? She'd be eleven in August. No matter how hard Evelyn tried to pretend Maisie was still a little kid, she was proud of her daughter's compassionate heart. Bewildering emotions to go along with all the other confusion in her life.

Maisie frowned as she handed the phone back. "She can't. Her dad's working and she has to help her mom with the little kids."

Evelyn tried to be sorry but couldn't find the words. Instead, she took Maisie's hand and swung it as they walked the few blocks to the apartment.

They changed into their swimsuits and added shorts and tanks over top. Evelyn loaded her backpack with towels and water then they cycled across town. Blocks of housing gave way to acreages with larger homes nestled amid the streaks of volcanic rock. The natural grasses and sage were already yellowing in the July heat, but patches of green showed where residents irrigated their lawns and gardens. They pedaled north on Rim Drive and dismounted at the pull-out for the swimming hole.

A black truck rumbled toward them then stopped, idling. Ben Kujak leaned a tanned elbow out the driver's window. "Hey, going for a swim?"

"Yep!" called Maisie. "It's sooo hot. Are you coming, too?"

Evelyn's cheeks warmed, if that were even possible. The air temperature must be pushing one hundred, if not more.

His gaze settled on Evelyn for a long moment. "I wasn't planning to. I live just up the road and was on my way home."

He lived out here? Who was this guy, really? How could running a food bank pay him well enough for one of these fancy acreages? This area wasn't prime farmland, but still.

"Have a great afternoon!" Evelyn called back. She pushed her bike down the trail toward the creek.

"You, too."

She wouldn't have looked back except she didn't hear Maisie behind her. "Maisie?"

Damp hair stuck out below her daughter's helmet as she stared at Ben. "Aren't you hot? The creek is the best way to cool off."

No doubt he rode in an air-conditioned truck to his air-conditioned house. He didn't need a swimming hole.

"Not today, thanks."

Evelyn's gaze swung to meet his. His words may have sounded casual, but the look in his eyes was anything but. The intensity took her back a step. What was that about? He couldn't be... aware of her, could he? As in, attracted?

His face melted into a half-grin. Rueful, perhaps.

She pulled her focus to her daughter. "Maisie, come on. I'm boiling here."

"Okay. But you should try it sometime, Ben. The creek is just the right amount of cold. It feels really good."

"I'll keep that in mind. Have a good swim, and be careful when you cannonball off that rock, okay?" His window rose smoothly. He lifted a hand in a wave and drove away. Almost immediately, his left signal light came on, and he turned off Rim Drive.

"Huh. He must've swum here if he knows about the rock." Maisie pushed her bike past Evelyn. "I don't know why he would rather be hot than go swimming with us."

He must've swum here if he lived next to the swimming hole. Not that Evelyn was about to point that detail out to her daughter. Strange Maisie hadn't seemed to notice. "He probably has air conditioning."

"Yeah, but swimming is better. More fun."

Given her choice, Evelyn would take both. By the time they pedaled back to the apartment, they'd be just as overheated as they were right now, but spending time at the creek with her daughter was worth it, either way.

She followed Maisie the rest of the way down the trail. "Some people also prefer quiet time alone without other people around them." Ben seemed like he might be that kind of guy. A loner.

Maisie swung to look at her, a horrified frown on her face. "That's just weird."

Evelyn laughed. "There are a lot of people like that in this world. Start watching out for them. You'd be surprised."

Her daughter leaned her bike against a rock and shrugged out of her clothes. "Bet I'm wet before you." She took a flying leap off the big rock and landed with a resounding splash.

Chapter 6

EN STOOD IN THE tiny commercial kitchen at Corinna's Cupboard and sautéed several pounds of ground beef in a giant stockpot. A dairy farmer had donated an entire old cow's worth of the meat, claiming it had no commercial value.

He believed it. There was little flavor, but it *was* protein. It had also been free, not to mention already portioned into one-pound frozen bricks wrapped in brown paper. He could deal with those.

Maybe tonight he'd skip eating here and fix himself something when he got home. Something fresh. Tasty.

Reaching for a giant can of pasta sauce, he paused. Was he better than the people he served? No, but he did have more resources at his disposal. Money. A home. Not enough to take care of forty people on his own, though.

Evelyn had offered him fresh vegetables.

He'd turned her down. It had been a reasonable thing to do. Right?

Several bags of iceberg lettuce, two days past their best-before date, sat in the refrigerator. He'd have to pick out any brown bits and slimy edges. Would it really be that much more work to wash garden-fresh greens?

A sharp knock on the back door got his attention. He set down the can opener, turned off the burner, and opened the door.

A tall guy about his own age stood on the other side cradling a paper bag of French bread so fresh the yeasty aroma teased the air.

Ben's mouth watered and his stomach rumbled slightly, certainly not a reaction he'd had while starting the pasta sauce for tonight.

The guy thrust out one hand. "Hi, I'm Jonah Baxter from the new bakery in Arcadia Valley Shopping Center. A Slice of Heaven? You may have heard of it."

Ben hadn't, but if the fragrance in the air was an indicator of what he'd been missing, he'd be at their front door on a regular basis. He shook the man's hand. "Ben Kujak, operator of a soup kitchen."

Jonah's face crinkled into a smile. "So I've heard. Our primary business model at A Slice of Heaven is bread subscriptions."

What on earth was that? Ben's brow furrowed.

"Basically people set up standing orders. They might want one French loaf—" he lifted the bag "—and a sourdough rye every Thursday, for example."

"Uh, that sounds great, but I don't have much of a budget. Most of the bread I serve here is a day or two old and is donated from the Food Mart or the Gas n' Shop."

"Oh, I wasn't asking you to buy a subscription. Our

church started the greenhouse project for Corinna's Cupboard. My siblings and I haven't been able to get involved there — too busy — but we've been blown away by the support in this town, and we're looking for ways to give back." Jonah thrust the bread at Ben. "Please accept this. I hope you can use it."

Ben stared at the four rounded golden ends protruding from the bag. "This is amazing. It's pasta night. You've made about forty hungry people really happy."

The other man frowned, jutting his chin at the offering. "Is there enough?"

"More than. I'm a bit overwhelmed, actually."

"How often is pasta night?"

"Every second Wednesday."

Jonah grinned. "I'll see you in two weeks then with another delivery."

"You don't... you can't..."

"Why not? God is blessing our business, and we want to pass it on."

"Well, when you put it that way..."

"Exactly. Hey, didn't I see you at Grace Fellowship last Sunday?"

Ben nodded. "Yes. I usually attend in Twin Falls but decided to check out a church closer to home."

"It was good to see you. We're new to town, like I said, but we've been impressed with how Grace is filled with people who want to make a real difference in the community. Plus, the preaching is solid."

"I enjoyed it a lot. I might be back." It might not be the teaching or the social outlook that drew him back, but the prospect of seeing a certain hardworking single mother.

"Good. I look forward to seeing you around." Jonah nodded once more then turned back to the small gray sedan parked in the alley. With a wave, he drove away.

Ben stood on the step, clutching the crinkly paper bag and filling his nostrils with the fragrance of fresh yeast bread. The unreformed backs of the buildings with revitalized storefronts lining Main Street stared at him across the alley with its broken pavement. The sounds of vehicle engines revved and quieted on the surrounding streets and a faint beep-beep-beep signaled a delivery truck in reverse. Above, several puffy clouds dotted the bright blue summer sky. A jet cruised overhead, its contrail an indicator of its past.

He took a deep breath and exhaled slowly.

It was good to be alive. Good to be in Arcadia Valley, making a difference. He didn't need to live in the fog. He could forge a new direction. His eyes followed the jet until it disappeared behind the building next door. The pilot was focused on where they were going, not on where they'd been.

Something like peace settled into Ben's emptiness as he watched the contrail drift apart. He returned to the kitchen and cleared a space for the bread at the end of the counter then picked up the can opener once again.

His mind drifted to Evelyn Felton. Their first meeting just down the hall, then at the church, lunch at the Sunrise, then seeing her and her daughter heading for a swim in the creek.

What was holding him back? Corinna had wanted him to be happy, and he didn't need to feel guilty for turning his gaze to the future. Five years was a long time to mourn what might have been. To wallow in his ache.

"Corinna?" It wasn't the first time he'd spoken to her aloud, right here in this kitchen that bore her name. "It's time, love. I'll never forget you. Never stop loving you, but it's time for me to move into my future." He poured the can of pasta sauce over the cooked beef and flicked on the burner. "God left me on earth for more than one reason, and I'm going to embrace that and seek out His gifts."

Ben closed his eyes, sensing the pivotal holiness of the moment.

Today, pasta and French bread for forty.

Tomorrow, Evelyn Felton.

"Hello?" A woman in a white chef's uniform stood in the doorway while kitchen heat and delectable aromas swarmed out around her. "Can I help you?"

Huh. So chefs really dressed like that, not just on TV. Evelyn smiled. "I'm looking for Ms. Taylor."

"I'm Morgan Taylor." The woman's narrow eyebrows rose. "And you are...?"

"I'm Evelyn Felton. Someone told me you might be—"

"Hiring? I'm sorry. You'll need to go in the front and ask for an application."

Heat flared up Evelyn's face. "No, thank you. That's not why I'm here." Though she'd guess L'Aubergine wait staff made excellent tips. "I'm wondering if you ever buy produce from locals. I have a truck with lettuce—"

"We're all about buying local, honey. It's what we're

known for, but our vendors are in place." Morgan reached for the doorknob.

"I have heirloom podded peas," Evelyn dogged on, "and the snow peas are just beginning."

The other woman narrowed her eyes. "How many peas?"

"A five-gallon bucket today. Probably the same amount on Saturday."

"May I see?"

Evelyn dared a breath. Maybe her hare-brained idea to go from one restaurant to another would work after all. Ben might have refused the produce from the gardens, but he could still use the money. Even if all it amounted to was enough to buy a new file cabinet. How had she ever thought she could manage such a big project? She knew so little about food.

Except what it was like when there was too little. When an innocent child suffered. She knew that side all too well.

Morgan popped open a pea pod and expertly extracted the small green balls. "Nice and sweet." Her fingers scooped through the top layers. "How much for the bucket?"

Evelyn's brain froze solid. "I, uh, what's the going price?"

The chef pulled back and studied her. "I'm trying to understand why anyone would grow this many peas—" her wave took in the entire backseat of Evelyn's old car "—lettuce, what have you, without knowing the market or having an outlet in place."

"It's a long story."

"Short version, please."

"Grace Fellowship is operating the old Akers Garden

Center greenhouses near downtown as part of a living trust. The purpose was to provide Corinna's Cupboard with food for the hungry, but the manager doesn't have volunteers in place to handle fresh produce. So now I'm trying to sell it so we can donate the money. This was never meant to be a for-profit venture."

"Ben Kujak." Morgan's head was shaking as her lips pursed. "That man doesn't know how to ask for help. Okay, so basically you're looking for a donation for this bucket of peas." She reached inside a deep pocket and held up a checkbook. "Who do I make this out to? You or Ben?"

"Corinna's Cupboard. And thank you."

The chef grinned as she made short work of scrawling out the check. "Ben can thank me later." She tore out the paper and handed it to Evelyn. "I have all the lettuce I need. Really, our suppliers stay very on top of things, but I could use fresh peas."

Evelyn stared at the check. Five hundred dollars? That couldn't be right. She met Morgan's gaze. "This..."

"Is a donation to a registered charity. Don't worry. I'll write off the excess." Morgan reached for the bucket. "If you wait a sec, you can have the bucket back. I'll dump the peas in a sink and put our kitchen help on it right away."

Evelyn barely had enough time to tuck the check in her folder before Morgan was back. "Any ideas of a restaurant that might take the lettuce?"

The chef thought for a moment. "Have you tried El Corazon, the Mexican place? It's a few blocks closer to the highway." She pointed.

"No, I haven't been there yet. Thanks for the tip."

Morgan laughed. "Not sure if it's a tip. Until recently, they've offered pretty old-school Mexican fare, but I hear they're freshening the menu. Can't hurt to try. Ask for Alex or Javier."

"Thank you." Evelyn took the empty bucket from Morgan. "I really appreciate it."

"My pleasure. Ben Kujak needs all the help he can get, even if he doesn't think so."

Sounded like someone who'd known the man a while. Evelyn slid back into her clunker as Morgan closed the kitchen door behind her. Down a few blocks, she could see the red tile roof of the Mexican restaurant.

Dear Lord. Thank You that Morgan bought the peas. I pray You'll allow the lettuce to find favor as well. Ben's face drifted into her mind's eye. *Please bless Ben and all he does to help the homeless and hungry, and thank You that I have three jobs and am not dependent on Corinna's Cupboard for our daily food.*

She might not enjoy all three equally, but that wasn't anyone's fault. Creating events for the town and doing billing for a group of dentists kept a roof over their heads.

Just as she turned onto the street, her cell phone rang. She glanced over, but didn't recognize the number. Evelyn pulled against the curb and picked it up. "Hello."

"Evelyn?"

Her heart skipped a beat. "Yes, this is Evelyn. Who's calling?" But she knew Ben's voice, even if she didn't know his number.

"Ben Kujak. Listen. I've been thinking."

What could she say into the silence? "That's always a good start."

"Yeah." He chuckled. "Can we talk? About vegetables, I mean."

Why had her heart surged then plummeted? What else did she want from Ben Kujak? Oh, she knew. He was a mystery, but one she desperately wanted to solve.

Desperately? Really, Evelyn?

"Evelyn, are you there?"

"I, uh, yes, I'm here. We can discuss vegetables."

"Great. When's a good time for you to swing by Corinna's Cupboard? Or we could meet somewhere and talk over coffee."

"What's your schedule like? I'm free for the next hour or so." She'd put the lettuce in the back room at the greenhouse for a while. It was as cool a place as any. Maybe she wouldn't need to try to sell it to El Corazon.

"Great. I could meet you at The Jukebox in fifteen? If that works for you?"

"Sounds good. See you there." Evelyn flicked off the call and stared at the device for a moment.

Fifteen minutes? What was she, some kind of crazy? She probably looked a hot mess — no, she'd dressed nicely and done her hair and makeup for her rounds of restaurant kitchens. She was fine. She just needed to offload the lettuce so it wouldn't sit in an overheated car while she...

Talked about veggies. But, still, it was a start, right? Ben'd watched her every bit as much as she'd watched him on Sunday at the Sunrise. He might've been chatting mostly with Grady, but his eyes had swung to her at every lull.

Maybe only because he'd felt her gaze on him. Because she'd had a hard time not staring at his shock of light brown hair, the animation overtaking his chiseled face, the light in his startling brown eyes.

Stop it, Evelyn. Don't waste your entire fifteen minutes daydreaming.

She shifted the car into gear, rounded the block, and drove back to the greenhouse. Thankfully no one was working there mid-morning on a Thursday. She didn't have to explain her jerky movements as she hauled the lettuce into a cool spot then dashed into the restroom to make sure she looked okay. Not that she had time for a change of clothing or a makeover.

Okay. Game on.

Chapter 7

BEN ROSE AS EVELYN entered the front door of The Jukebox. She looked amazing in a lacy green top over a solid green skirt swirling just above her knees. Heeled sandals pivoted as she turned to scan the diner.

He waved, and a smile lifted her face as she came toward him. His mouth went dry. Why on earth did he want to talk about vegetables or the needs of Arcadia Valley's homeless with a gorgeous woman? He should be taking her to a movie instead.

She slid into the red-and-white vinyl booth and set her oversized purse down beside her.

A waitress in a poodle skirt and bobby socks bounced over. "Would you like menus?"

Ben sat across from Evelyn. "You hungry? Maybe a piece of pie?"

"No, thanks." She smiled up at the waitress. "A glass of iced tea, please."

"I'll have coffee. Black," Ben put in.

"Sure thing."

He watched as Evelyn looked everywhere but at him. The realization hit him. She was nervous, too. Somehow that put him more at ease. "How has your week been going?"

She shot him a quick glance. "Busy as always. Juggling three jobs and trying to keep Maisie occupied until school starts in a few weeks. She spends a lot of time at the gardens, waiting to pounce on any weed that dares poke through."

"Three jobs?" Ben couldn't keep the surprise out of his voice.

The waitress set the drinks on the gray laminate table.

Evelyn bit her lip and toyed with the straw in her glass. Ice cubes clinked. "Together they make up about thirty hours a week. This week, a bit more."

Was that his fault? "One of them is managing the garden, right?"

She nodded. "Coordinating the volunteers. Making sure we have the needed supplies." She sipped her iced tea, still not making eye contact.

"Trying to get rid of the produce," he said quietly.

"Well, yes. The farmers market doesn't have space for drop-ins." Evelyn's face brightened. "But I was at L'Aubergine just before you called and she took all the peas we had picked. Which reminds me..." She dug around in her purse then slid a piece of paper across the table. "Here."

A check for five hundred dollars made out to Corinna's Cupboard? Signed by Morgan Taylor? Ben frowned and pushed it back. "But..."

"It's for you."

"But I can't..."

"Why not? Fifty-three volunteers have been growing vegetables for your charity for three months. Not being able to donate the actual produce doesn't change the purpose of what we're doing." She hesitated. "I know now I should have come by and talked to you earlier. It's been busy, and it never occurred to me that it would be a problem."

He didn't deserve this from her. How could he accept?

Evelyn's subtly pink fingernail caught the edge of the paper and nudged it a few inches to his side of the table.

His hand reached out and covered hers. How had that happened? He stared at her tanned fingers peeking out beneath his thicker ones, his skin warm where it touched hers. Alive. "I... uh..."

She tugged free and wrapped both hands around her glass of iced tea. Her pretty face flushed and her eyes looked anywhere but at him.

"Evelyn."

"It's okay, Ben. Don't worry about it. You wanted to talk about the veggies? I still need to find a place to take the lettuce we picked last night, so go ahead. Tell me what's on your mind."

"How many heads?"

She blinked. "How many heads what?" Her gaze caught on his for a brief second.

"Of lettuce."

"It's a mix of leaf varieties. There are about eight kinds, I think. Different textures, different flavors, different colors.

Morgan suggested I try selling them to El Corazon."

Ben looked at the check still lying on the table. "I can't believe you're doing this."

Her gaze snapped to meet his and her jaw tensed. "What am I supposed to do? I have an entire bin of lettuce. It would be a waste to compost it all."

"I'll take it. I'll take everything you've got."

"But you don't have help. You don't—"

"I'll take them, Evelyn. It's no fair, you going to all this extra work to help out Corinna's Cupboard when you have a daughter and two other jobs." She probably wasn't getting paid for the extra time.

"But—"

"I messed up. I should've trusted God to send me the help I needed along with the food."

Her eyebrows rose and her face brightened. "You've found volunteers?"

"No, not yet. But I didn't really ask Him, either. I was stuck in a rut, doing what I've been doing for the past few years."

Evelyn searched his face. "Then why the change of heart?" A blush blossomed on her cheeks as she looked down. "Change of opinion, I mean."

She'd been right the first time. "A few things, I guess. I've become aware that I was beginning to look at Corinna's Cupboard as my thing, not as God's thing or even that of the people I serve."

When she toyed with the edge of a paper napkin, he reached over and covered her hand again, drawing gentle circles on her thumb with his own. Her hand stilled, and her startled gaze met his.

"You've helped me become aware of those things... and more."

Her lips parted and then closed. Still her brown eyes looked into his own.

"I need to know. Are you seeing Cameron? Or anyone else?" Of course there could be someone else.

She shook her head slightly. "No. There's just Maisie and me. I-I haven't been looking for anyone. Just trying not to fail at this parent thing."

Ben laced his fingers with hers on the tabletop. "You're not failing. I've never met a more focused and compassionate kid. My guess is she learned it from you."

"I'm not sure about that."

"I am." His fingers caressed hers. "So, if you're not dating anyone, would you consider going out with me? I'm attracted to you, Evelyn. Your beauty and your caring spirit. I'd like to get to know you better."

"Maisie..."

"Would she mind, do you think?"

"I don't know. We've never talked about... things like... that."

Somehow this didn't seem like the right time to ask about her child's father. "Would you and Maisie like to come out to my place Sunday after church? Spend the day?"

Evelyn pulled away and wrapped both hands around her glass as she took a long sip through the straw.

She needed a moment. He could understand that, even if he wanted her eyes to light up as she offered a breathless yes. He'd had a bit of time to think this over, but she'd had little warning that he was headed this direction.

"Are you going to the church movie night in the park tomorrow?"

He blinked. "Grace Fellowship? I did see that in the bulletin Sunday, but I'd forgotten all about it. Are you and Maisie going?"

Evelyn nodded. "She's been hyped up ever since they first announced it a few weeks ago. She's getting a bunch of her friends together."

Wait. Friday night. Corinna's Cupboard. "How long will it run? It's a soup kitchen night."

"The picnic starts at six, and the movie at seven."

If he left the dishes undone and went back in on Saturday, he wouldn't miss much of the movie. It was some animated kids' flick, if he remembered right. Not his usual thing. But the chance to spend a bit of time with Evelyn before Sunday? Definitely priceless.

Evelyn loaded her plate with a hamburger and potato salad then added a pile of the greens she'd donated from the greenhouse project. Ben had said the amount was more than he could use, after all.

"Mmm, Nancy Poncetta's fried chicken," Grady's sister Kenia murmured behind her in line. "You need to try some, Evelyn. It's the absolute best."

Fragrant spices rose from the golden pieces, but Evelyn had already added condiments to her burger. She angled her plate so Kenia could see.

"That's no excuse." Kenia dropped a drum beside the burger. "You need to at least try a bite. It's the only reason I came to this picnic. You, too." She swiveled and deposited a piece on Joanna's plate behind her before setting two on her own. "You'll thank me later."

Joanna chuckled as the three of them made their way back to the old quilt Kenia had spread earlier. "So how was your week, ladies?"

"Aunt Irene turned me loose on ordering more local interest books for the store." Kenia smiled smugly. "You know Arcadia Valley was smack dab on the Oregon Trail, right? I found some history books that mention those who left the wagon trains here, like Granddad's grandparents."

"Oh, that's interesting." Evelyn glanced around. It was too early for Ben to arrive, wasn't it? But she didn't want to miss him, just in case.

Joanna bumped her knee against Evelyn's. "Who're you looking for?"

"Um, just seeing who's here that I recognize. Looks like we have a lot of visitors." She waved at Ruth Baxter, who strolled by with her fiancé and her brothers. "It's a great outreach."

"What have you been up to?" Joanna tipped her head to one side and narrowed her gaze. "You look like the cat who captured the proverbial canary."

"No canaries. Don't even give Maisie the idea of a bird for a pet."

"Where is Maisie?" Kenia strained to look around. "I can't imagine her missing movie night."

"No. She's here, hanging out with Kaleena Espinoza and

some of their other friends. She's almost eleven, you know. Too old to be seen with Mom in public."

"Ha." Joanna snickered. "That'd be the day. Nothing fazes her, that one."

Not so far, but how would she react when she discovered her mother was considering a boyfriend? Wow, hadn't a better word been invented yet? Evelyn had boyfriends in high school. Even though Ben looked young, he was in a whole different league.

A completely new and captivating league. A tiny smile turned up her lips.

"Have you noticed anything different about Evelyn?" she heard Joanna stage-whisper.

"No, what?" Kenia matched the voice.

"I think she's in lo-ove."

Evelyn blinked her friends back into focus. "Give it up, you two."

"True, though. You said something about meeting Ben for coffee yester—"

"Ben?" interrupted Kenia. "Ben who?"

"Kujak. You know, the guy who runs Corinna's Cupboard."

"Oh, him." Kenia turned to Evelyn, eyes wide. "He's brooded for years. Do you mean to tell me he is actually waking up to smell the roses? And I missed it?"

"Where's Grady? I thought he was meeting you here?" Anything for a change of subject.

Joanna took a bite of coleslaw. "He said he would. He was expecting a shipment of flowers late in the afternoon and thought he'd get away late. How about Ben? Isn't he coming?"

"The soup kitchen is open Fridays." Evelyn clapped her hand over her mouth.

"So is he coming later?" Joanna's eyes twinkled.

"I think so. If he doesn't have anyone who needs to stay late to talk. You won't make it hard for him, will you? You won't tease him or anything..."

"Joanna is probably too nice, but I'm not. Wow, seriously? Ben Kujak?" Kenia's eyes grew wide as she looked past Evelyn. "There he is now. Looking for you, probably." She waved.

Why couldn't Founders Park be prone to sinkholes? Evelyn could use one about now. Why had she ever thought meeting Ben at a public event was a good idea when they hadn't even dated yet? All she'd thought of was Maisie off with other kids. She'd thought it might come across like a casual meeting. She hadn't counted on her friends.

"Hi, Evelyn. Hi, Joanna. Kenia." Ben's voice came from directly behind her.

Evelyn angled her head to look up at him. "Hi yourself. You got out of there earlier than I thought."

He grinned. "I left the dishes for morning. Didn't want to miss out on a great meal made by someone else. Or the latest blockbuster movie."

Kenia snickered. "Oh, definitely on the movie. If you adore talking animals, you've come to the right place."

"Sounds good." His gaze lingered on Evelyn. "Where do I pay up for this feast?"

"Over by the pavilion." She held up her hand to display her yellow bracelet. "You'll get one of these fashion accessories, and they'll turn you loose on the food."

"I'll be back in a few. Save me a spot?"

She nodded, mouth dry, as he strolled away.

"Well, I'll be hot-jiggered," Kenia breathed. "Joanna's right. Ben Kujak is alive and well on planet earth. How did you *do* that, girlfriend?"

Evelyn poked at her potato salad. "I didn't do anything. We just met a couple of weeks ago over the greenhouse project."

"And fell in lo-ove. I can't believe this. First my brother." Kenia pointed her finger at Joanna. "An avowed bachelor for years. You waltz into his life and he's suddenly all soft and mushy and adorable. And now Ben. I need some of that Kool-Aid."

"It's guy Kool-Aid." Joanna chuckled. "It'll put hair on your chest, and I don't think you want that to happen."

"Okay, fine. I want to be the first woman some tall, dark, and handsome guy sees after he drinks a gallon of the stuff. Is that better?"

"My brother is tall, dark, and handsome."

Kenia rolled her eyes. "Puh-leeze. Cameron is so not my type."

Over by the pavilion, Ben and Grady ran into each other with a mutual back-slap then turned toward the lineup, yakking away. All Kenia's joking aside, was this really happening? Evelyn'd had a hard time sleeping last night for the jittery feeling in her gut as she remembered the intensity of his eyes and his fingers twined with hers at The Jukebox.

If this was Kool-Aid, it was mighty powerful.

Chapter 8

"WHY ARE WE GOING to your house, Ben?" Maisie asked from the backseat of the truck. "Can we go swimming?"

Evelyn had packed their swimsuits just in case, along with Maisie's Summer Reading Club books. If her daughter got really bored, there were always a few games on Evelyn's phone. Just like her daughter, she had no idea what to expect.

Ben watched Maisie in the rearview mirror, a grin poking at the sides of his mouth. "If you want."

"You live by the creek, right?"

He nodded.

Why couldn't Maisie just wait and see? They turned onto Rim Drive, passed the swimming hole trail, then left into a driveway.

Evelyn shifted in the passenger seat, as eager as her daughter to see what lay ahead. Here the volcanic rocks peeked through wild grasses already turning yellow in the summer heat. They rounded a curve to see a two-story house across from a small barn built of native rock. A rail fence beyond the barn enclosed a—

"Ben!" shrieked Maisie. "You have horses!"

Evelyn rubbed her ear. She turned in her seat as the truck coasted to a stop beside the house. "Settle down."

"But, Mom! Horses. Three of them."

A brown and black dog rose from a mat on the covered porch, stretching and wagging.

Maisie squealed. "Oh, you have a dog, too? You're so lucky. Can I pet him?"

So much for worrying about her daughter getting bored while Evelyn and Ben sipped iced tea in the shade.

Ben chuckled. "Gypsy's a girl, and yes, you may pet her."

The truck's backdoor opened and slammed shut behind Maisie. She ran up the steps and crouched in front of Gypsy. The dog bounced to lick Maisie's face.

Ben turned sideways in his seat. "Welcome to my place, Evelyn."

She glanced at him as she tucked a strand of hair behind her ear. "Th-this isn't really what I expected." But what had that been? Was it so weird he had a real home?

"I've lived here seven years."

With his family, then. It still seemed strange to think he'd been married. A father. He looked too young for so much love and so much loss. "It looks... idyllic."

"Really?" He glanced around as though trying to see it as she did. "I like it here. Just minutes from town. Quiet."

Evelyn's dreams had only been big enough for a house instead of an apartment. Some of Arcadia Valley's rentals had yards big enough for a garden and a pet. She'd never allowed herself to imagine anything like this.

She still wouldn't.

With a start, she realized Ben had come around the vehicle and opened the door for her. He caught her hand and helped her down from the tall truck. "Want the tour?"

She took a deep breath. "Sure."

"Mom, look!" Maisie's face was wreathed in glee. "Gypsy likes me. I want a dog. Where did you get her, Ben?"

"Do you know Riley Jennings? She runs a boarding kennel for dogs. Paying customers and a few rescues." Ben turned to Evelyn. "Have you met her?"

"She has a booth at the farmers market selling dog treats, doesn't she? I've seen her there." How could she not? It was Maisie's favorite meeting place.

"That's her. I don't know where she finds all the animals in need of rescue, but she is sure enthusiastic about introducing them to new homes." A pensive look crossed his features.

"She seems like a lovely person." Evelyn bent to rub Gypsy's silky ears. "I don't know her well. It's not like we can have a pet in the apartment."

Maisie burrowed her face in Gypsy's shoulder, and the dog licked the girl's hair. Maisie giggled.

Ben cleared his throat and sent a questioning glance to Evelyn. "I heard you might like horses."

Her daughter's head bounced up. "I love horses. Only I've never been near one."

"We can change that right now. Want to come over to the corral and meet Rapunzel?"

Maisie angled her face so she could look at Ben without letting go of the dog. "Can Gypsy come, too?"

"Sure. She hangs out with the horses all the time. They get along."

"Oh, good." Maisie jumped to her feet. "Come on, Gypsy!" The girl and the dog ran ahead toward the barn.

Evelyn's heart hurt for her daughter. She could see Maisie thriving in a place like this. A dog. Horses. Who knew what else? What if this thing with Ben didn't work out? What if she'd given her daughter a glimpse of the way other people lived and then had to snatch it away from her?

She glanced at Ben only to find him watching her.

His fingers wrapped around hers. "She looks happy."

"Pretty much her dream come true, but maybe you couldn't tell."

Maisie climbed onto the lowest rail of the corral and leaned over, Gypsy's paws planted beside her sandals. "Hello, horses." She glanced over her shoulder, not seeming to notice how closely they stood together. "What are their names?"

A large brown horse ambled closer to Maisie, snuffling her hair.

Maisie giggled.

"That's Penny." Ben leaned against the fence beside Maisie and pointed to the shade of the barn. "Over there is Halim. See how his tail is flicking flies off both of them? The pony's name is Rapunzel."

"Because she has long hair..." breathed Maisie. "She's beautiful."

Bad idea. They shouldn't have come. Maisie's heart was going to be broken when all this was taken from her again. Even now the girl's eyes shone with awe.

Ben whistled, and the pony perked up and trotted over. "If you pull a handful of tall grass and hold it between the fence rails, she'll probably come to you."

"C'mere, Rapunzel," crooned Maisie as she stretched out a clump of grass. "You're so pretty."

The pony nipped the greens carefully from Maisie's hand then searched for more.

Maisie beamed at Ben. "She likes me. Can I ride her?"

"Now, Maisie..."

Ben's shoulder pressed against Evelyn's as he leaned closer. "It's fine by me," he said quietly. "I can walk them around the paddock for a few minutes. Unless you want to ride, too?"

She stepped back. "I've never ridden."

"Would you like to?"

His warm brown eyes held an invitation to more than a horseback ride. She didn't dare think what else. "No, thanks. Not today."

Ben's gaze held hers. "How about Maisie?"

Evelyn grasped the top rail with both hands and nodded. "If you're sure. If you stay right with her. She knows nothing."

His finger grazed her cheek. "I will. She'll be fine." Then he vaulted the fence and strode toward the barn door, all three horses trailing behind him.

Half of Evelyn gasped with relief that he no longer looked at her, spoke to her, touched her. And yet that feather-light touch awakened more in her than she'd guessed lay dormant. Something she wanted to explore. Could she really find happiness with Ben? A future?

Thankfully, Maisie had been content with a twenty-minute amble around the paddock. Ben had stayed nearby — he'd promised Evelyn, after all — but Maisie was a natural. She'd listened to every word he said then did her best to follow his advice. Now she flopped in the shade of the giant pine in the backyard, Gypsy sprawled next to her.

Ben came out of the house with a tray of iced tea and reheated burritos from El Corazon.

Evelyn rose from the Adirondack chair on the back deck. "May I use the restroom?"

"Sure." He'd made sure the house was clean, knowing she was coming. Seeing his office in disarray was bad enough. He didn't want her to think he lived that way, because he didn't. He set the tray down and held the door ajar, pointing. "Right through to the other side, just off the front entry."

She strolled through the living room, her graceful form swaying slightly in the long tan shorts and turquoise and tan polka-dotted top that hugged her curves.

Ben took a step back and collided with the door that had shut behind him. She wouldn't appreciate being ogled like he was a teen high on hormones. Those hormones had taken a nap for a few years. He wasn't sure whether to thank them for reappearing or not. So long as they didn't master him, they might be a good thing.

His gaze strayed to the framed photos above the mantle. He should've put away the central family portrait, or at least the one on the right of him and Corinna gazing into each other's eyes. The one on the left, of three-year-old Zoey, was likely fine. Ben took a step closer. He should swipe the couple picture and stick it behind the sofa, even though the arrangement would obviously be off center.

Before he could reach for it, the restroom door reopened and Evelyn came toward him. "Hey, you found everything okay?" Mentally, he kicked himself. Duh. She'd been in the correct room.

"Yes, thanks." She glanced around the space. "Nice home you have here."

He tried to see it with her eyes, the big windows to the backyard, the lava rock fireplace, the leather seating and the man-cave-sized television. "Thanks. We... I like it." He edged toward the TV, hoping her gaze would follow.

Evelyn turned to the fireplace. She sucked in her bottom lip as she looked from one portrait to the next.

Ben closed his eyes. What had he been thinking, inviting her here? Why hadn't he thought of the pictures this morning when he'd whisked the feather duster across the place?

"Your family?" she asked softly.

He swallowed hard and stepped up beside her. "Yes. Five years ago, not long before the accident." Corinna's parents had booked the photographer for an extended family gathering. Corinna had chosen her favorite poses and had them framed.

"Your little girl looks very sweet. What was her name?"

"She was." Ben's throat closed. "Zoey."

"Was Rapunzel her pony?"

"Yes. Her grandparents bought her the pony for her third birthday. Too young, really, but we loved to ride."

Evelyn clasped her hands behind her back as she angled her head to one side and gazed at the portrait of him and Corinna. The room was so quiet he could hear the fridge humming in the kitchen. The clock ticking on the wall. What was she thinking?

"You look very much in love," she said at last.

"We were." To say otherwise would be lying. "Two kids who believed in a happily ever after, but it wasn't to be."

"Ben? Are you sure?"

He turned toward her, leaning against the fireplace. "Sure about what?"

Evelyn's gaze flicked past him to the portrait then back to his face. "About inviting me here. Me and Maisie."

He reached for her hands, but they stayed clasped behind her back. "I won't lie and say it's not an adjustment to my thinking. After Corinna and Zoey died, I was numb. I was angry at God and poured everything into charity work in Corinna's name. It's only recently that I've begun to believe in second chances. Realized that God didn't make a mistake in keeping me alive that night."

"Were you with them? What happened?"

"We met at her parents for dinner in Twin Falls. I'd been at work — I worked in construction back then — and she'd driven in later with Zoey, so we had both vehicles there. I followed her home." Ben paused, blinking back the memories.

"It's okay." Evelyn's fingers rested on his arm. "You don't have to tell me."

"I want to." He gripped her hands with both of his. "I saw the accident. Saw the white pickup slide into her lane. Drunk driver. Icy roads. There was a crash." He'd hit the brakes, swerved into the ditch, and run for Corinna's car. Even now, when the nightmare struck, it was all in slow-mo, like he was attempting to run through chest-deep water. He couldn't get there in time, but it wouldn't have been enough even if he had. Corinna's body was crushed, mangled, but she knew he was with her.

"I'm sorry, Ben. It must have been horrible to be right there. Did she... was she already gone?"

He shook his head. "I called 9-1-1. They brought the Jaws of Life. I held onto her through the smashed window while we waited. But it was too little, too late."

She'd told Ben she loved him and to find happiness... and slipped away.

"And Zoey?" whispered Evelyn.

"She lived three more days." Then joined her mama in glory.

"I can't imagine what you've been through. How hard it must have been."

This wasn't a conversation he'd anticipated having so soon, but maybe it was better this way. Get everything in the open. He searched Evelyn's eyes. "What about Maisie's father? What happened to him?"

She pulled her hands away and stepped back. "I have no idea."

So she hadn't enjoyed an idyllic marriage. He and Corinna had been young, granted, but they'd been solid. Devoted to each other with every fiber of their being.

Evelyn brushed past him and out to the deck. She stood at the railing, shoulders hunched slightly. Trembling.

Ben followed her. He glanced around for Maisie, but she was throwing the Frisbee for Gypsy, not paying any attention. He stepped close behind Evelyn and braced his hands beside hers on the rails, his chest lightly brushing her back. "Evelyn?"

He felt her shuddering breath. "What?"

"Tell me."

"I wasn't sweet and innocent like you were. Hormones went too far one night after a football game. I was sixteen."

"I wasn't so innocent. Corinna was, but not me. My parents split up when I was fourteen. My mom left with my sister, and my dad started drinking really heavily. In my mind, everything was his fault, and I detested him. Couldn't stand being around him, so lots of nights I didn't go home. Couch-surfed at friends' houses, slept on a park bench or two." He'd been so full of bitterness. Wasted so much time. So much effort.

Evelyn started to turn. He stepped back to give her room then shifted closer again. That tenuous contact — he needed that. To know someone heard his words, felt what he'd felt.

"Is that where you learned compassion for the homeless?"

Ben shook his head, grimacing. "No. I guess, if I thought of them at all back then, I assumed they were avoiding home like I was. I know better now, of course, but I was a selfish teen."

"Did you and your dad mend the situation?"

"Not really. He's remarried, and I see him occasionally. I just can't bring myself to pretend those years didn't happen."

Evelyn looked down. "I get it. I wish I didn't, but I understand all too well."

Ben lifted her chin with the tip of his finger. "I'm sorry you understand. What a pair we are."

Her gaze flicked to meet his.

"I thought you said there was gonna be food. I'm hungry." Maisie's plaintive voice came from right beside Evelyn.

Those burritos would need reheating. Again.

Chapter 9

*B*EN PEERED INTO EVELYN'S BASKET. "I thought you said you had peas."

"I did, but L'Aubergine is taking them all." Right, Morgan had given another donation. Evelyn dug her clipboard out of the car parked behind the food bank. "And here's her check to Corinna's Cupboard."

"She needs to stop doing this. It's far more than the peas are worth." Ben shook his head. "I was looking forward to a taste."

"I'm sorry." Evelyn stopped and stared at him. "I never thought... you said..."

"I know." He ran his hand through his hair and gave her a lopsided grin. "But I haven't had fresh peas in a really long time."

"Come by the greenhouse. They'll be picking again tomorrow, and you can certainly help yourself to a few handfuls."

"They? Where did you find all those volunteers, anyway?"

Evelyn chuckled. "I wasn't kidding when I said Maisie rounded them up. She took flyers to the various churches plus stuck them on power poles and bulletin boards around town. And she spoke up in her school assembly. Lots of people were curious about the greenhouse project and joined in."

"But that was months ago."

"I know. I've been amazed, too. I thought we'd have more dropouts."

"So I need to ask your daughter to find me some cook's helpers?"

Evelyn chuckled. "She'd do it, too. How many do you need?"

"Man, even one volunteer for a couple of hours on the days the soup kitchen is open would be amazing. Did I tell you that the new bakery is donating their day-old bread now? If we got their *week*-old it would be a dozen times better than the pasty mush we'd been getting from Food Mart."

"I thought they did subscriptions."

"They do."

"Then how do they have leftovers?"

"They bake extras and sell it out of their storefront. Have you been in there yet?"

She shook her head. While a bread subscription sounded like the slice of heaven declared by the advertising, it wasn't likely in her budget. "My life revolves around lettuce and peas. Tomatoes just coming on. Green beans." She flashed him a grin. "Organizing volunteers."

"Don't rub it in."

"Look, I have half an hour right now. Do you want some help?"

"You sure?"

"Why not? Is it okay to leave the car in the alley?"

Ben nodded. "Just lock it up. It'll be fine." He hoisted the basket of lettuce out of the backseat and carried it into the kitchen.

Evelyn followed, stopping in the doorway. "This is very compact."

"Are you afraid to be near me?" He smirked at her as he set the lettuce down.

Her eyebrows rose. "Should I be?"

She took a step closer, and her brown eyes caught the light like wells of molten chocolate. They darkened as Ben reached for her waist and tugged her closer. Her world tilted as he swept one finger down her cheek.

"You're the best thing that ever happened to me," he murmured.

Ever? But she didn't question him. She was too lost in his intense gaze as her hands grasped a fistful of his T-shirt, feeling the thud of his heart. So alive. So real. "I know what you mean."

"Evelyn," he murmured, lips on her forehead. He gathered her tightly against his chest, one hand splayed against her back, the other massaging her neck through the tangle of her hair.

Her arms slipped up over his shoulders, and her fingers toyed with the fringe of hair at the nape of his neck as she pressed her cheek to his strong chest. She hadn't thought she'd find herself falling in love, but the peace she felt in Ben's arms, even with emotions and tantalizing touches zinging between them, couldn't be anything else. And why not? He was a man of faith, a compassionate man, free to love her back. His wife and daughter were gone — had been, for a long time.

She'd never had such ties. What had gone down behind the bleachers that night long ago with Buck had never been love. She'd known it even then, but she'd kept her distance from the male species ever since. She didn't need a repeat.

Ben wasn't that kind of man. Even now he held her like a fragile treasure, his lips barely nuzzling her forehead, yet awakening a desire for more.

Evelyn leaned back ever so slightly, breaking the contact, and looked into Ben's eyes. Her lips parted at the intensity and focus in his gaze.

He lowered his mouth to hers, gently claiming her. Her eyes drifted closed as she reveled in the sensation of his lips while she eagerly kissed him back. Her fingers tightened in his hair, and she felt his hands caressing her back, her waist, her neck while their lips discovered each other.

She'd watched as the bean seeds they'd planted in tiny peat pots poked through the black dirt, every day a little taller, the tight heads unfurled a little farther every time she checked. Sacred love was sprouting here in this charity kitchen, just as seeds in the greenhouse had sprouted, grown, stretched for the light. Now those same bean plants clambered over trellises in riotous abandon, white flowers giving way to tiny pods that would soon be mature enough to harvest.

Was it silly comparing this feeling to the seeds she'd been working with for months? Those little seeds held all the promise of the full-grown plants.

She kissed Ben, imagining this new love sprouting, unfurling, growing, popping flowers... becoming all it was meant to be as it reached for the sunshine.

"You're amazing," he whispered against her mouth. "I don't deserve you."

She didn't deserve love, either. Did anyone? But he hadn't said the word, and she wouldn't be the first. Did the tiny seed sprouting through the soil know it was going to be a bean plant? No. There was time. Time to nurture this relationship with the equivalent of sunshine and rain and experience its growth.

His hands slid to her waist. He kissed her once more then leaned back a little, a bemused expression on his face. "Wow. I wasn't expecting this."

Evelyn allowed a lopsided smile to emerge as her fingers slid across the frayed neck of his T-shirt. "Me, either. Thank you."

Ben took a deep breath and let it out slowly, the movement of his chest pressing against her. "Much as I'd like to keep kissing you — and believe me, I would — I have forty people coming for dinner in just under an hour. I probably ought to start cooking."

"What's on the menu?"

"Something new for me."

Her eyebrows rose. "I thought you had a rotating meal plan."

"I do. But life's been a bit off-kilter lately, so when the produce manager at Food Mart offered me a few bags of peppers that were starting to get spots on them, I took a chance and accepted."

"Mmm. Sounds like fajitas."

"Great minds think alike. I had some terrific ones at a friend's house the other night." His finger trailed down her jawline again. "I'll have to take you to El Corazon sometime. Amazing Mexican food."

She stretched in for a quick kiss then pulled back. "Sounds great, but I bet yours will be just as good. Want me to slice peppers?"

"I'd like that. But I doubt mine will be up to their standard. I got Food Mart to donate a few foil envelopes of spice mix while they were at it. I'm pretty sure Javier Quintana doesn't buy generic seasoning for the restaurant."

"Maybe not." How would she know? Eating out was something she did rarely. She could be thankful she wasn't at the receiving end of Corinna's Cupboard. "Peppers in the fridge, I assume? How about a knife?" She eased out of Ben's arms. Time to get started.

Ben's gaze kept swerving to where Evelyn stood preparing peppers and mounding the colorful arcs into a large bowl. He sliced a slab of beef into thin strips. He should've started sooner so the tough meat would've had time to marinate, but he hadn't. He couldn't regret the minutes he'd spent kissing Evelyn. Not when she'd kissed him back like he'd been dreaming of lately. He shot another glance in her direction.

She'd tied her long hair back at the nape, exposing the side of her face to his gaze, her forehead, her straight nose, her full lips, her chin, her graceful throat...

His knife slipped. Ben jerked back just in time to avoid slicing his finger open.

"You okay?" Her brown eyes caught his, and her forehead furrowed into a slight frown.

"Just distracted." He grinned at her. "But I didn't cut myself."

Her gaze flicked to his hands then back to his face. "Good. Blood on food is never advised."

"What did I ever do without you in my life?" He set the knife on the cutting board. Safer that way.

"Does that require an answer?" She sliced the core out of a red pepper and deftly removed a black spot.

"Maybe?"

She shot him a glance. "Maybe what?"

"Maybe it requires an answer." He didn't want to cook tonight. He'd rather kiss Evelyn some more, but forty people expected food in half an hour, and enough pizza was out of the budget.

Ben turned back to the meat. Nearly done. He could focus. "What I did without you in my life was spend a lot of time sitting around wishing things were different. I'm not proud of that."

"You were hurting," she murmured.

She gave him more grace than he deserved. "Yes. That was acceptable for a time." How long was long enough to grieve a lost wife and child? No doubt it varied from situation to situation. For him, though... after a while, he'd wallowed instead of embracing life. Not that he should've looked for love again sooner. Not that. But engaging in activity. Being part of his community. Seeking out friends.

What would he have done without Felipe? Their friendship had been all Felipe for the longest time. Even now, he still accepted his friend's weekly visits without much effort on his own part. Accepted that Felipe needed to escape his house and five daughters with a guys' night out and play mindless video games.

Needed to escape? That was crazy. Felipe worked long hours as a police officer, and he had a good marriage with Constance. He coached girls' softball and attended his daughters' dance recitals. Felipe didn't need out of his house. He was just the kind of guy who quietly stepped into the gap and didn't budge.

Ben shook his head as he massaged the spice mix into the meat.

"I'm done with the peppers. Where do you put the compost?"

He stared at her blankly and washed his hands. "Compost?"

"The scraps." She pointed at the pile of membranes and seeds.

"I, uh... the garbage can is in the corner." He cringed. That was not the answer she was looking for.

"You don't separate out the compost?" Her hands landed on her hips.

Ben ducked his head. "Sorry." He dug out a giant wok and poured oil into it.

"I'll get you a bucket, and you can either drop it off at the greenhouse a couple of times a week or I can pick it up. All these food scraps break down and feed the soil. They don't belong in the landfill."

"No. You're right. I just never thought about it." He gave her his best puppy-dog eyes. "Sorry?"

"I expect you to do better in the future." A little smile teased at her eyes and lips, belying the stern words.

"I will. I promise. I can't stand being in your bad books."

Evelyn smirked. "You have no idea what that's really like. Ask Maisie."

"Do you ground her?" He scooped a bundle of meat with a pair of tongs and dropped them in the sizzling oil. "I could stand it if you were there, too. Maybe you'd kiss everything better." From the corner of his eye, he caught the motion as she shook her head.

"Silly."

"Would you? Because I like kissing." *Focus on the hot wok, Ben.*

"It wasn't so bad. We could try it again sometime. You might not even have to beg too much." She leaned against the countertop beside him, arms crossed, facing him.

"Don't distract a man while he's cooking, woman."

"I wouldn't dream of it." Her grin widened.

Ben chuckled and leaned over to press a soft kiss on her lips. "I think you'd better get out of the kitchen, because I can't stand the heat."

She tilted her head, eyes twinkling. "I remember that saying a bit differently."

"It's true both ways." He waggled his eyebrows. "Don't you have a salad to prep? Someone donated greens, I think."

"Oh, you want me to *stay* in the kitchen. I misunderstood."

He snapped the tongs in her direction. "If this meat burns, I blame you."

"Maybe you should turn down the heat." Her eyes simmered.

It wasn't a bad idea. He twisted the knob slightly and angled away from her. Later. Later he'd kiss her senseless and make her regret taunting him in his own kitchen. Or maybe neither of them would regret it.

Chapter 10

MOM, CAN I GO TO day camp at Bigby Farm? Kaleena's going next week."

Evelyn leaned back in the office chair at the greenhouse. "No, sweetie. I've told you before. We can't afford it."

"But you have three jobs."

Was she gone too much? She'd been so careful to keep her hours regular and only when Maisie was occupied with friends or at the greenhouse. She'd even limited time with Ben since last week. There hadn't seemed to be a good time to let her daughter know she was falling in love.

"Even all together, they're not the same thing as one job, and none of them pay really well." Grace Fellowship paid the best, but couldn't make up for the piecework she picked up planning town events like the upcoming harvest festival or billing for the dentists.

Maisie crossed her arms in front of her, lower lip jutting out. "It could be my birthday present?"

How Evelyn wished. She shook her head. "Don't even start, missy. We're doing a lot better than we were, but money doesn't grow on trees." But she did need to start planning something for Maisie's eleventh birthday. To think her baby would be off to middle school in just a few weeks. It hardly seemed possible.

A door clicked over in the greenhouse.

Evelyn rose and held her hand out to her daughter. "Come on. Let's see what's happening."

Maisie shuffled out of the tiny office ahead of her.

"Hi there!" Joanna waved from over by the shelving unit. "I wasn't sure if anyone was in today."

"Yes, I'm here, trying to unravel another knot of red tape for the after-school program." Evelyn set her hand on Maisie's shoulder, but her daughter slouched away. "Just when I think bureaucracy has been appeased, I discover another layer exists."

"Isn't that the way." Joanna grimaced. "Now I know why Arcadia Valley has a perpetual shortage of daycare spots. I never really thought about it before moving back here and sharing Cameron's care of the twins."

"I could babysit them." Maisie looked from one adult to the other.

Joanna slung an arm across Maisie's shoulder. "Don't I wish. They get in so much trouble they practically need an adult each. Preferably one with six eyes."

Evelyn noticed her daughter didn't dislodge Joanna's touch immediately.

"They'd behave for me." Maisie's jaw set.

"If you were thirteen, we'd hire you in a minute, but you're ten."

"Eleven in two weeks." She glared at Evelyn.

Now her age was her mother's fault, too? "There are lots of good things about being not-quite-eleven."

"Name one." Maisie ducked away from Joanna, who gave Evelyn a puzzled look.

"You get to ride your bike all over Arcadia Valley. The twins are way too young for that."

Maisie's eyebrows flickered.

"You get to boss around a bunch of adults out at the garden beds. Don't think I haven't heard you," Joanna added with a grin, nudging Maisie's shoulder with her fist.

"That doesn't count."

Joanna leaned against the sales counter and crossed her arms as she gave her attention to Maisie. "You do know you're making a bigger difference to this town than ninety-five percent of the adults, don't you?"

Maisie shrugged.

"The meals at Corinna's Cupboard have improved," Evelyn added. "You got Ben a couple of volunteers, plus the tomatoes and beans are coming on now."

"Yeah. That's cool. But what about just being a kid?"

"Since when did you want to be a kid?" asked Joanna. "I thought you were born changing the world. Most kids don't think about things like you do."

"I want to ride horses." She shot a look at Evelyn. "By myself, not being led in circles in a dinky corral."

"Where did that happen?" Joanna looked confused.

"Out at Ben's. You'll get another chance, Maisie. Once you prove to him that you're comfortable on Rapunzel, you'll be able to ride."

Her friend's eyebrows shot into her hair. "At Ben's? I think I'm behind in the news."

Maisie crossed her arms. "We went there on two different Sunday afternoons. He only lets me ride for a little while, but he's not paying attention while he helps me. And I don't even need help."

He'd asked if he could also saddle up Penny and Halim last week, but Evelyn had demurred. She'd never ridden and wasn't sure she wanted to start right now, on Corinna's horse. Maybe she'd been being selfish. It obviously meant more to Maisie than she'd realized.

A grin flickered on Joanna's face. "He's not paying attention to you at all, huh? What's he doing?"

"Jo—"

"Just curious."

Maisie sighed. "Talking to Mom."

"Oh, what are they talking about?"

"I don't know. Vegetables maybe. I try not to listen."

An unladylike snort erupted from Joanna as she turned to Evelyn. "Oh, that's too funny. You and Ben talk about *vegetables*?"

It did sound weird when put that way. "About food, anyway. He's a good cook."

Joanna grinned. "He's cooked for you?"

"I'm not sure why you're making such a big deal about it." Evelyn held her friend's gaze and tipped her head toward Maisie. "We're friends."

"She kissed him," announced her daughter. "She thought I wasn't looking."

Oh, no. "Maisie!"

Joanna sucked in her lips as her eyes danced with suppressed laughter. "That does put a different spin on being friends."

"Okay, enough talk about Ben." Evelyn pointed a glare at Joanna. "Did you come down to the greenhouse for anything specific?"

"Just hadn't seen you for a while. Now I know why. Too busy for your other friends."

"You've been busy, too." Her friend wasn't going to pin everything on her. "Planning a wedding and all."

"Not that much to plan yet." Joanna swept the words aside with a hand glimmering with a large diamond. "We've booked the church and the reception hall. We're trying to decide on caterers. Grady wants Demi's Delights, and I was thinking El Corazon. Which do you think has the greater appeal to guests, Greek food or Mexican?"

Evelyn held up her hands. "I'm not getting involved. Both are great options."

"I'd think my maid of honor would care a little more."

"Your... *what?*"

"Maid of honor. Will you stand up for me, please?"

"Me? Seriously? What about Grady's sister?"

"I like Kenia, but we're not super close. I've asked her to be my bridesmaid. I don't want a lot of attendants. Just you two. If you'll say yes."

"I. Wow. I'd be honored. I never expected—"

Joanna squeezed the breath right out of her. "Well, you

should have. Because you're definitely my closest friend here in Arcadia Valley, and I don't want anyone but you beside me."

"And Grady."

"Definitely him on the other side." Joanna sighed, a dreamy smile on her face. "I can't believe I'm lucky enough to be marrying the man of my dreams."

"Weddings schmeddings." Maisie rolled her eyes.

Evelyn watched her daughter traipse into the greenhouse. "Let's hope her opinion doesn't change for the next decade or two. I'm dreading the day she discovers boys."

Her friend looped her arm over her shoulders. "You're a good mom. You and Maisie will do fine. And long before then, you'll have a good man at your side to help with the teenage shenanigans."

Ben. Please, Lord, let it be Ben.

"At least, if the rumors I've heard about kissing are to be believed."

"There may have been some. Once or twice." A day. For a week.

"Good." Satisfaction colored Joanna's voice. "I'm so happy that I want the same for my best friend."

"I brought snacks." Felipe kicked off his sneakers beside the front door. "If I wanted sliced peppers and dip like last week, I'd eat what Constance buys at the farmers market."

Ben swiveled his chair around and raised his eyebrows.

"It was a Tex-Mex dip. Thought your Latino taste buds would get all giddy over that."

"You thought wrong. Constance's is much better, and she lets me eat chips with it, not just carrot sticks." Felipe set his grocery bag on the counter and held up a bag of pretzels mixed with cereals and nuts. "Now *this*, my friend, is how party snacks are done. First these." He dumped some into a bowl. "Then chips. Good Stargil ripple chips. And a basic ranch-style dip. Nothing weird. Nothing with eggplant or zucchini in it." He reached for another bowl, but there weren't any a similar size in the cupboard. Felipe shrugged and dumped the potato chips on top of the pretzel mix.

Ben laughed. "You're weird."

Felipe pointed the dip container at him. "No, my friend. *You* are the strange one. I am here to reset your taste buds before I have to revoke your man card. What's it going to be?"

"Pretty sure I have an artichoke dip in the fridge. Want to try some?"

"No." Felipe set the containers on the coffee table. "Thank you, but no. Can I get you a can of pop while I'm up?" He turned back to the kitchen.

"Just water for me."

Felipe pivoted. "Now that is taking this whole thing too far. Water? Seriously, my friend?"

Ben couldn't hold the laughter back any longer. "A cola is great. Thanks. Had you going for a minute, didn't I?"

"Am I to believe the artichoke dip was also a joke of some sort?"

"Nope. There's really some on the second shelf. Totally

edible on rice crackers."

"I am not sure which is worse, a Ben who spends all his time moping or one who thinks eggplant is amusing." Felipe grabbed two cans and handed one over. "I'm hoping the new Ben is as easy to wipe out in this post-apocalyptic game as the other one."

"I think I'll win tonight, if it's all the same to you." Ben slid the game into the console and nudged a controller around the bowl of chips at his friend. "Are you ready to go down in a hail of bullets?"

"No. I think not. You will have to earn every hit." Felipe waggled his eyebrows. "Game on."

Ben played with an aggression he'd forgotten he had, smearing Felipe two games out of three. "Yes! That's more like it." He reached over and smacked Felipe's hand, which had not exactly been raised to receive a high-five. "What're you going to do about *that*, man?"

"Nothing tonight. I demand a rematch next Thursday. Then we will see who's boss."

"I'm on a roll. It won't make any difference."

Felipe dragged the bowl of chips closer. "So this new Ben. The one who eats strange snacks and yet kicks butt in video games. That one."

"Hmm?"

"This must have something to do with that woman you met a few weeks ago. The one you refused to talk about last week."

Was he ready to let anyone into his world? Into his happiness? If not the man who had stood beside him in his darkest hours, then who?

Ben snatched a handful of party mix with a few chips. "Maybe."

Felipe raised his eyebrows. "Either there is a woman or there is not."

"There's a woman. Evelyn."

"And she is the one responsible for the vegetables?"

Ben nodded. "She's the coordinator of the Grace Greenhouse project on the old Akers property. Growing food for the charity."

"I thought you told her no. That it was too much work."

"Then she went and sold them to Morgan Taylor at L'Aubergine and Morgan wrote Corinna's Cupboard a check."

"Win-win."

"You'd think. Maybe for Morgan and her customers it was. But not for Evelyn. She was putting in a lot of extra time peddling the produce."

Felipe raised an eyebrow.

"So she found me a couple of volunteers, plus she comes in herself one afternoon, and we're making good use of the food. Now *that* is win-win."

"So Evelyn is one of your helpers."

Ben smirked at Felipe. "She is."

"Does that make it a triple win?"

"It might qualify." He took a sip of his cola, now lukewarm, and eyed his friend. "Felipe, do you really think this is okay? I haven't told Corinna's parents I'm seeing someone. I don't know what they'll say."

"It isn't really any of their business, is it?"

"Maybe not, but they are in charge of the charity, so I

work for them. They could make it difficult for me if they wanted to."

"Why would they want to? It is not like you and Corinna divorced. They set up the foundation to honor their daughter's memory, though I'm not sure I ever learned why they chose a soup kitchen. Was this something Corinna had talked about?"

Ben rose and walked over to the window. "She was obsessed with trying to find my mother," he said at last.

"Pardon?"

"My mother went to Alabama to connect with some guy she'd met online and took Bryanna with her. Only he wasn't the dependable steady person she'd assumed from their chats. He was a user. An abuser." Ben turned to look at Felipe. "When she realized she'd been had, she contacted my father, but he wouldn't accept her back. He did buy a plane ticket for Bryanna."

"What happened to your mother then?"

"I have no idea. I can't find a trace of her online, either as Kujak or her maiden name." He shook his head. "Corinna was sure Mom ended up on the street somewhere. She may be dead, for all I know. It's been almost fifteen years."

Felipe crossed the room to stand beside him. "Have you hired a private investigator?"

Ben blinked. "It never entered my mind. I thought if she was alive she'd turn up on Facebook sooner or later. Doesn't everyone in the English-speaking world have an account?"

"I do not. Constance does. She plays Candy Crush, I think it is called. I would rather waste my time chasing down post-apocalyptic treasure hunters in your living room."

"Me, too. How much does a PI cost?"

"Depends on how long it takes. A routine preliminary search would not be excessive. Do you want me to look into it for you? I can let you know."

Was he ready to take this step? "Yes, please."

Chapter 11

*E*VELYN LOCKED UP her office in Town Hall. Plans for the Harvest Festival in October were coming along. The Boys from Boise had confirmed the Saturday night concert, and the Forkful food truck would be on the premises all day Saturday, serving Delis sausages on rolls from the new bakery.

She checked her watch. Ben had been so enthusiastic about A Slice of Heaven, yet she'd never gone in. She was due to meet him in an hour — after Maisie got back from an afternoon visiting elderly Clarence Akers at Retro Village with Joanna and the twins — to go out to his place for supper. Maybe a baguette or something wouldn't go amiss. Between the leftover produce at the greenhouses and so many meals with Ben, she actually had a little more money than month for the first time in living history.

After locking her bike in the rack at Arcadia Valley Shopping Center, Evelyn headed into A Slice of Heaven. One of the Baxter brothers smiled at her from behind the counter.

"Is Ruth in today?"

The man shook his head. "No, I'm afraid not. She's booked solid at Fairview B&B this week. You're Evelyn Felton, right? From the greenhouse?"

"Yes, that's me. I've seen you at Grace Fellowship, I believe?"

He nodded. "Jonah Baxter. Nice to meet you. Can I interest you in a bread subscription?" He launched into an explanation of how it worked.

Evelyn's gaze caught on the pricing on the chalkboard beside the window. As she suspected, out of her range. "No, sorry," she said ruefully when she could get a word in edgewise. "All I need today is a baguette, or something like that. What do you have?"

"Over on this side. Not a lot left this late in the day, sorry." The bell over the door tinkled. Jonah glanced up, and a bemused smile crossed his face.

Evelyn glanced over her shoulder to see Gloria Sinclair, one of the local police officers, heading to the sales counter. Another peek at Jonah confirmed her suspicion. "Actually, one of those sourdough olive breads look really good."

Jonah blinked and looked back at Evelyn. "Uh, the kind with sundried tomatoes or the kind without?"

"Which do you recommend?"

"Depends what you're having with it, I guess."

Made sense, but Ben hadn't told her what was on the menu.

"They're both amazing," said Gloria from behind her. "Such rich flavors. You can't go wrong with either one."

Jonah flashed a smile at the police officer.

Far be it from Evelyn to stand in the path of new love.

"I'll take one with tomatoes, please. And thank you."

Stepping outside a moment later, she inhaled deeply of the dry summer air. The aroma of yeast bread joined it. The whole world seemed full of sparkles and dancing unicorns this week. Even the baker and the policewoman seemed to notice.

A cloudless blue sky arched over the town she'd grown to love. Arcadia Valley had simply been a random dot on the map when she'd left Tennessee three years before, but it had become the home she'd never had. The one connection had been Teri Blackstone, who had some ties to the area and had noticed online that the town was hiring a part-time events manager.

The sign for Benita's Gourmet Market caught Evelyn's eye from a few doors down. She had time. She'd check that little shop while she was in the area.

Ben pulled up in front of the shabby building where Evelyn and Maisie lived. A few portable A/C units protruded from windows, but not, he knew, in Evelyn's second-floor apartment. He'd only spent an evening inside once, and the place was stifling.

He beeped the locks on his truck as he jogged up the steps. The doors were propped ajar, nullifying the security system. He grimaced. Yes, Arcadia Valley was a small town with a low crime rate, but this just seemed to be asking for trouble. He made his way to the back of the building and tapped on the door to #208.

Maisie swung the door wide. "Hi, Ben."

He stepped into the overheated living room. "Hi, beautiful. Are you and your mom ready?" If not, someone would be collapsing from heat stroke. Maybe him.

"Almost!" called Evelyn from down the short hallway. "Maisie, did you open your bedroom window? Let the place air out a bit while we're gone."

"The screen's broken, Mom."

"Oh, right. I told the manager, but he hasn't been by to replace it yet. Better leave it open anyway, or it will be too hot to sleep tonight."

Ben opened his mouth in protest. An open window, especially at the back of the building, was nothing but an invitation for burglars. Or worse. Though maybe burglars wouldn't think there was anything of value in this neighborhood.

Maisie trudged into her room at the end of the hallway, and Ben heard a window rolling. "It's still hot out there."

Evelyn appeared, tucking an earring into one dainty lobe. She flashed him a grin then turned to Maisie. "I know. But we'll get a bit of a breeze soon. It's worth it. You ready?"

How could she look so impressive and so put together with her limited financial resources? Evelyn never ceased to amaze him. Even in jean shorts and a tank top. He'd probed a bit about her background, but other than a few bare facts about her diploma from night school in Tennessee and Maisie's birth, she hadn't said much. Mind you, neither had he. The mess of his parents' lives was more than he wanted to divulge. Maybe it was time, though. It might encourage her to open up.

Evelyn closed the distance, and Ben couldn't resist slipping his arm around her waist and dropping a quick kiss to her soft lips. Beyond, Maisie rolled her eyes. Ben grinned. "Shall we?"

"Oh, I picked up something for dinner." Evelyn dashed around the corner into the kitchen and came back with a flat loaf of bread sticking out of a paper bag.

"Smells fabulous. What is it?" Ben peered inside.

"An olive loaf from A Slice of Heaven. You told me they were amazing so I stopped by there this afternoon. So many choices! It was hard to decide."

Evelyn pushed it into his hands, locked her door, and preceded him out to the truck, where he opened the passenger side for her. Maisie hopped in the back before he had a chance to open her door. A minute later he cranked the air and pointed the truck across town.

"What's for supper, Ben?" asked Maisie. "I'm starving."

"I was thinking we could grill steaks." He found her eyes in the rearview mirror. "Sound good?"

"Steak?" Maisie's face fell. "How about hot dogs?"

Evelyn made a strangled sound.

He chuckled. "I have some sausages in the freezer. Want me to get one out for you instead?"

"Yes, please. And a bun?"

"Sorry, I didn't pick up any fresh rolls. But it might taste good wrapped in a slice of this bread."

"I guess I can try that."

"Sounds like a plan." The town streamed by as he drove. Ben pointed out the window. "That's your new school, huh? Middle school already?"

"Yeah. It'll be weird being one of the youngest kids in school again. I like being one of the bigger ones."

He met her gaze in the mirror. "I can see that. You like to organize people, don't you? Just like your mom."

"Yeah. Older kids don't appreciate that so much."

"You'll figure it out soon enough. A born leader will find followers, no matter what."

"You think?" Her plaintive voice matched her eyes.

What? Maisie, vulnerable? Looking to him for reassurance? That was a first. "I know so. Maybe we can pray together this evening, and ask God to guide you and help you make new friends and figure it all out."

"Some of my friends will be in middle school with me. Like Kaleena."

"Kaleena?" Ben drove past the outskirts of town. "Kaleena who?"

"Espinoza. She's my best friend."

"No way." Ben chuckled.

Maisie's narrowed gaze met his in the mirror. "What's so funny about that?"

"Her dad is a police officer, right?" At her nod, he continued, "his name is Felipe, and he is *my* best friend."

"Really? That's weird. He seems like a nice dad."

These wistful words from a girl who'd never known a father. Maybe, just maybe, Ben would do something about that. The possibility had been poking at the back of his mind for a couple of weeks now. Would Maisie accept him in that role?

Ben glanced at Evelyn as he turned the truck onto Rim Drive. Would Evelyn?

Evelyn sautéed the first green beans of the season in Ben's kitchen. Through the sliding doors, he whistled a chipper tune, grilling three potatoes, two steaks, and one sausage while Maisie threw the rubber ball for Gypsy. Evelyn's heart was full. She could get used to this.

Ben stuck his head into the living room. "Almost ready. How about you?"

"One minute." She drizzled a few drops of lemon juice over the sizzling beans and garlic and stirred up the brown bits from the bottom of the pan.

Ben's arms surrounded her from behind. He kissed her, his stubble gentle on her cheek. His manly smell drifted to her senses, and she leaned back against his strong chest as she turned off the burner.

"I came in for plates," he murmured against her jawline, "but I got distracted."

"You wouldn't want to burn the steaks."

"I turned the grill off. They're fine." He turned her around and cradled her face between his hands. "Thank you." He kissed her slowly, softly.

"For what?" Evelyn whispered when she could find words.

"For being here. For being you."

She searched his face as her fingers gripped the front of his T-shirt. "Thanks for having us."

Gypsy yelped from the backyard, and one of the horses whinnied.

Evelyn chuckled as she stretched for another quick kiss.

114

"Time's up."

His hands rubbed her shoulders for a few seconds then he grinned, turned away, and pulled a tray from a bottom cupboard. Whistling, he added plates and cutlery before opening the fridge.

Evelyn transferred the beans to a serving bowl and found a spoon. She sliced the olive bread while Ben loaded butter and sour cream to the tray. They made a good team.

At first, she'd been overwhelmed by the ghost of Corinna in this kitchen, but that sensation had faded over the past couple of weeks. Besides, Ben had removed the portraits of his former wife from the wall above the mantle, leaving only the one of his toddler. If he'd transferred the others to his bedroom, Evelyn didn't want to know about it. She hadn't ventured into the private areas of his airy home.

After a delicious dinner on the back deck, they wandered hand-in-hand to the creek with Maisie and Gypsy running on ahead.

Then Ben said the words she'd once dreaded to hear. "Tell me about your family. You never mention your parents. Do you have siblings?"

Her fingers tightened convulsively around his. "My parents kicked me out when I told them I was pregnant."

Ben stopped stock still on the path, pulling her toward him. His arms encircled her, and concern darkened his eyes. "I'm so sorry."

"I was an only child." She lowered her gaze, watching the toe of her sandal scuff at the brown dirt. "I didn't measure up to their standards. So that was that."

"You never went back?" His voice was gentle.

"Never." She glanced at him then away. "But they never invited me, either."

"But you finished high school." The statement was more of a question.

She nodded. "A friend's family took me in. I worked as a waitress through the rest of my junior year to pay them for my room and board. Then during my senior year, Maisie's paternal grandmother watched her while I was at school. Much to Buck's dismay."

Splashing from the creek up ahead put motion back into Evelyn's feet. After they rounded the last curve and could see Maisie and Gypsy playing in the water, she perched on a black rock.

Ben sat beside her, shoulder to shoulder, fingers twined around hers. "That was good of them."

"I don't know what I would have done without them, honestly. After graduation, they encouraged me to go to college. Even paid my tuition. They knew it would be tough for a single mother, and they felt somewhat responsible for their son's actions."

"And Buck?"

She shrugged. "Went to a college out of state on a football scholarship. He never looked back."

"So that's when you got your diploma in business management?"

"No." Dark memories washed over her. Stopping at the house to drop Maisie off in the morning and finding no one home. She'd taken the toddler to class with her, but that hadn't gone over well. "Buck's parents were killed in a late-night pile-up on I-40. His uncle was a hot-shot sports lawyer and convinced me the courts would rule in Buck's favor if I tried to get child support. That I had nothing to offer Maisie, and I'd never see her again."

"Scum." Ben's voice was rough, vehement.

Evelyn took a shaky breath in and out. She'd let it go before. She could again. "It wasn't Buck's finest moment, I'll grant you that. I had two semesters of college left to go, but no money. No childcare." Her jaw clenched as memories overtook her. "No home."

Ben's arm wrapped around her, his hand rubbing her shoulder. "I'm so sorry that happened to you." His other hand covered her hands, clenched in her lap.

"But God was there." There had been light. Faint, like the first hint of dawn, but she'd focused on it. Clung to it. Believed in it.

"God is always there when we need Him the most." Ben's lips brushed her cheek. "What happened then? That was what, nine years ago?"

"Yes. Maisie had just turned two. We landed in a shelter alongside addicts and prostitutes. I couldn't do that to Maisie, but I had no choices, Ben. None."

The warmth of his arm around her back, the stroke of his hand on her arm, the pressure of his thigh against hers all served to ground her before the memories spiraled her down into a dark place.

"We spent two years on the street, warding off unwelcome advances, finding a night here and there in a shelter, lining up at soup kitchens, looking for something besides microwave macaroni and cheese on the food pantry shelves."

"Does Maisie remember?" he asked quietly.

The child and the dog romped in the water. Maisie scooped huge waves of water at Gypsy, who barked and leaped and tried to catch the drops. Both were soaked. Content. "She remembers more than I wish she did."

"That explains so much."

"Ben, I've been meaning to tell you what happened, but I was afraid you'd reject me. I'm not good enough to be in your life. I made such a big mess—"

"Sweetheart." His lips pressed against her cheek.

Evelyn blinked away tears, but they kept dribbling down her face. He kissed those away, too, while holding her hands captive.

"Evelyn Felton, you are the strongest woman I know, bar none. I've heard so many stories from homeless people. Many lose hope and stay mired for their entire lives, but you found God. You made it through."

"God and a mentor. A woman who worked for one of the churches in downtown Memphis paid for Maisie to be in their daycare. Teri taught some classes at the shelter on job searches. This church paid for countless women to get a decent wardrobe and hair styling and makeup. Helped us hone marketable skills." Teri's encouraging smile and words still prodded Evelyn out the door some mornings. "She believed in me, and she taught me to believe in myself. To believe in God's best."

"She sounds like an amazing woman."

"She was. With her encouragement and support, I went back to waitressing then to night school. It took another four years to finish my diploma. She even heard about the part-time job for the town of Arcadia Valley and encouraged me to apply. And here I am."

"It was God all the way."

"Yes. It was God, but He uses people. I'm so thankful for Teri. I don't know where I'd be today without her. Not here, that's for sure."

Chapter 12

EVELYN LEANED AGAINST the door to her apartment, listening to the rumble of Ben's truck fade away. They'd taken some huge steps forward tonight. He'd listened to her story and rejoiced with her that she and Maisie had made it through those awful years.

Maisie shrieked from her bedroom. "Mom! Mom!" But she sounded more excited than afraid. Evelyn hurried down the short hall.

Ben had insisted on checking for an intrusion when he dropped them off. So sweet of him, even though their windows had been open dozens of nights this summer. A screen wasn't going to stop anyone who wanted in, anyway.

Her daughter stood in front of her dresser, staring into an open drawer. "Can I keep her? Please with sugar and spice?"

Uh oh. Evelyn leaned over Maisie's shoulder and peered in.

A small orange cat crouched against a stack of folded pajamas, wide eyes swerving from Maisie to her then back.

"Sweetie, you know we can't."

"It looks hungry. See?"

Evelyn saw. The poor thing was so skinny its ribs rippled the striped coat, and its ears looked too large for its head. After revisiting that decade in Memphis, she felt a little more pity for the cat than she would've earlier. She knew what it was like to find what seemed a safe, out-of-the-way corner and then find people staring at her when she awoke.

"The building has rules." Even to herself, her voice sounded weak.

"The manager should have fixed the screen. How about if I leave the window open, and the kitty can leave if she wants to? I think I'll call her Tiger. She looks fierce."

They should put the cat outside, but Evelyn didn't want to touch it. The scrawny thing might attack, scratching and biting. Besides, it obviously knew how to get in and could do so again anytime until the screen was replaced. The manager was never in a hurry for any building repairs. They'd be lucky to have new screens by spring.

"Can I get Tiger a bowl of milk, Mom? Cats like milk, right?"

And then there was the matter of a litter box. Evelyn looked over at the wide-open window, a welcome cooling breeze shifting through the room and creating a flow through her own bedroom window. The cat could leave to do its business. And it did look gaunt. A bit of mercy never hurt anyone.

Evelyn sighed. "Okay. A little milk. And maybe we can open a can of tuna. But it can't stay, Maisie. You know that."

Her daughter squealed and flung herself at Evelyn. "Thank you, Mom. I'll take really good care of Tiger. I promise."

The cat scrunched further into the recesses of the drawer at the noise and movement.

Probably fleas leaped off their carrier and nestled into Maisie's clothes even now. Evelyn shuddered and her skin itched. "Only tonight, sweetie. When we shut the windows in the morning against the heat, the cat goes out. Promise?" It'd be too late for the fleas, but no doubt it already was.

Maisie wrinkled her nose and glared at her. "Fine." She flounced out of the room.

Evelyn heard the fridge door open and shut. "Hello, cat." She slowly stretched her hand toward the little creature.

The cat sniffed her fingers, wide green eyes fixed on hers. A low rumble filled the air.

Oh, man. The thing was purring. Evelyn had gone and made friends with it. She pointed a finger at the feline. "Don't get any thoughts of permanence, Tiger. Temporary solution only."

How many times had she heard those words or similar? She blocked them from her mind, turned on her heel, and made her way to the living room.

Maisie passed her carrying two small bowls and wearing a triumphant grin.

Evelyn flipped open her laptop and clicked on her email while listening to her daughter croon to the creature. She scanned the list of unread messages, and her gaze caught on Teri Blackstone's name. Funny to hear from her mentor tonight, just after she'd told Ben about the huge difference the woman had made in her life.

Dear Evelyn,

I hope this finds you and Maisie well. I'm glad to hear you were able to pick up a third part-time job with your church.

She'd emailed Teri months ago and told her about it. No doubt her friend was focused on another young woman in need right there in Memphis, doing what she did best... not checking email.

Arcadia Valley is a lovely town, and it makes me happy to know it has been good to you. Having the third job must make all the difference in the world to a sense of permanence. It gives me heart and hope as I continue to minister to homeless women — like I once was — and help them get on their feet, as my mentor did for me.

Evelyn sat back. That's what made Teri such a terrific sounding board. She'd been there. She'd known exactly what Evelyn and her other charges needed.

I'd love to see a picture of you and Maisie in your new setting. How she must have grown! I'm thrilled to hear your faith is strong. If I may, I'd like to offer one more word of advice. Perhaps two. Always remember Jesus, the author and finisher of your faith. Cling to Him always, Evelyn. And if He brings a godly man into your life, be willing to consider the possibilities.

I can't tell you how much God blessed me when He introduced me to George. Not only did George love and accept me, knowing my past, even the ugly divorce that sent me to the streets, but he's enabled me to help others. Partnered with me. So, don't push the thought away. God loves His children and wants to complete their lives.

Best wishes, Teri

How could her mentor be reading her mind from all those miles away? Knowing that it was hard to think of a full and happy future with Ben? They'd known each other over a month now. Taking it slow. Neither had said, "I love you."

Okay, it didn't feel slow, even with that omission. It felt like she was hurtling through space, but it was wonderful. He was good with Maisie, and Maisie seemed to like him in return. Although... maybe the attraction was more Gypsy and the horses. Either way, Maisie was thrilled to spend a few evenings a week out at the acreage.

Evelyn had revealed her soul to Ben tonight, and he'd murmured understanding and sorrow for her sake. Had God brought him into her life to complete her, to partner with her, as Teri had said?

Her heart sang with the prospects.

Ben settled into his usual chair in the Martinez media room while Max hooked up his laptop to the 60" TV.

Fran bustled in with a tray of coffee and dessert. "I made the lemon squares just for you, Ben. I know they're your favorite."

He smiled up at Corinna's mother as he helped himself. "Thank you." Would she still be making his favorites after tonight?

Voices came from the TV as Corinna's siblings honed in from their distant homes. "Hi, Ben." Darla's fingers fluttered as the webcam revealed the Martinez home to the virtual visitors.

"Hi, Darla. Maxwell." Would either of them be on his side? Ben's knee started to jitter of its own accord, and he shifted his weight in the chair to suppress his nervousness.

"You're ready to take minutes, Darla?" asked Max, taking his seat around the curve from Ben. Fran settled between them.

"Sure am, Dad. I'll type them as we go along and email them to all of you later this evening."

Like she did every time, but the conversation always took the same course at the beginning.

"All right. Let's open this board meeting with prayer." After a short invocation, Max turned to Ben. "Go ahead, then. Tell us what's new in the past month at Corinna's Cupboard."

"Thanks, Max. The biggest change is that one of Arcadia Valley's churches, Grace Fellowship, has taken the charity under their wing. The main way they've done this is by planting and tending gardens and then donating the produce to the soup kitchen."

Maxwell steepled his hands on his half of the TV screen. "It sounds like their heart is in the right place, but the means are not so practical. Am I correct?"

"That's definitely how I felt at first. Then the project coordinator began to give the produce to local restaurants for a donation to the charity." Ben turned to Fran. "I dropped off those checks to you a couple of weeks ago."

"Two checks for five hundred dollars each from L'Aubergine. Max and I went for dinner there after the second one, just to see what they're all about. One of the finest dining experiences we've ever had."

Ben hadn't ever eaten there. It seemed too much of a

disconnect from his work with the homeless, but maybe sometime he'd take Evelyn.

"Wow, that's a lot of money," Darla said. "Sounds like a win-win to me."

"Yes and no. The homeless people for whom all those volunteers were growing the food weren't receiving it. But yes, the funds went a long way to restocking the pantry shelves."

Maxwell leaned closer to his webcam, his face looming on the screen. "You said *at first*, Ben. Does this mean the project isn't ongoing, or am I reading too much into the words?"

Ben nodded at his former brother-in-law. "Good catch. Yes, things have changed. The project manager was putting a lot of time into finding a different outlet for all the produce meant for Corinna's Cupboard. I joked that she should simply volunteer to help cook at the soup kitchen instead."

Maxwell's eyebrows rose.

"So, that's the change. She comes in one afternoon a week, while several other members of Grace Fellowship help on the other days."

"That's wonderful, Ben!" Darla's face lit up. "I've been worried about you doing everything yourself, but it's been hard to offer any practical assistance from Boston." Her gaze shifted to her parents. "And I know Mom and Dad are so busy with the real estate office and providing the day-to-day direction you need. To say nothing of all the fundraising."

Ben glanced sideways at Max and Fran. "There's no way I could do what I do without them."

"I have a question," offered Maxwell from his home in

Chicago. "What you're doing is wonderful, Ben. Don't get me wrong. But is this really what you want to do for the rest of your life? I know looking out for the underdogs was Corinna's passion, but she's been gone five years now. Are you continuing on because of guilt, or is this truly what you believe God wants you to do on an ongoing basis?"

Ben sensed his brother-in-law wasn't finished, so he waited.

"I don't mean to be insensitive. I loved my baby sister and was thrilled to see her so happy with you. I'm just wondering if maybe it's time for you to move on."

Here went nothing. Ben leaned forward, resting his elbows on his knees. Hopefully the pressure would keep his knee from doing a nervous dance on its own. "I think you're asking two separate questions, Maxwell."

The other man's eyebrows rose. Darla's head angled on the screen as she gave him her full attention. In Ben's peripheral vision, Max and Fran turned toward him.

"Do I believe Corinna's Cupboard is my life's work is the first question. Even a few weeks ago, I couldn't have answered that. You know I've been drifting. Just hanging on to the familiar, doing the same thing every week. Putting in time."

Darla's lips parted as she leaned in to say something.

Ben held up his hand. "It's true. You suspected it, and I knew it. Sure, the charity is making a difference. You all are a huge part of that behind the scenes. Raising funds. Offering direction. Running the legal bits." He nodded to Maxwell. "Thank you. That leads to the second part of your question."

Maxwell's eyebrows pulled together. "Go on."

"Which was if it's time for me to move on, personally." Ben closed his eyes for a second. *Lord, give me words.* "I loved Corinna and Zoey with everything in me. Please never, ever doubt that."

Beside him, Fran murmured something.

"But while I feel that I'd like to continue with the charity — so long as you are all in agreement — I-I've met someone." He cast a sidelong glance at Fran and Max. "I think you'll really like her. I hope and pray you will."

Fran dabbed at her eyes with a tissue, and Max slid his arm around his wife. "Is she someone we know?"

Ben shook his head. "I don't think so. Her name is Evelyn, and she's a single mother. Her daughter, Maisie, will be eleven next week."

"A single mother?" asked Maxwell. "Where is the child's father?"

"He's never been in the picture. You also need to know that Evelyn's parents kicked her out of the house when she was sixteen and pregnant. She spent several years on the streets in Memphis, and it was through a place like Corinna's Cupboard where she met a mentor who introduced her to Jesus and helped her complete a diploma in business management. She now works part time for the town of Arcadia Valley as an events manager and part time for Grace Fellowship overseeing the garden project for Corinna's Cupboard."

Fran hurried from the room, the tissue pressed against her face.

Ben's heart sank. Should he have spoken to her alone, earlier? Even though all the relationship they had left revolved around the charity, he should've thought of the blow his revelation would be to her.

Darla was the first to find words. "Good for you. It's about time you found someone again. When's the wedding?"

Ben stared at the screen. "Early days yet. I felt you all should know before things progressed much further. In case it made a difference to you."

"I can see why you'd like to stay with the charity," said Maxwell. "You have a new infusion of energy and understanding for the needy. Seeing as how Mom left the room... Dad, do you think this is a problem? A conflict of interest in some way? Does Corinna's Cupboard need to find someone else to run the project in Arcadia Valley?"

Max's gaze flitted to the doorway, across Ben, and back to the screen. "I'll need to speak with your mother and get back to you on that."

Ben turned in his chair, focusing on Max. "Are you saying that you cannot give your blessing to me falling in love with a woman who loves the Lord with all her heart? Corinna's gone. I was never unfaithful. I never would've been. You know that."

"I know." Max looked down at his clenched hands. "Still, it may be a problem. We need time to consider the implications."

Chapter 13

THE FARMERS MARKET TEEMED around them as Evelyn steered her daughter toward Riley Jennings' booth. Maisie's reluctance — obstinacy, really — was etched in every line of her downturned mouth and every slouch of her matching shoulders.

"Sweetie, you know we can't keep the cat."

Maisie's shrug dislodged Evelyn's hand. Her daughter wouldn't forgive her anytime soon, that was for sure.

"—tastiest treats you'll find anywhere and made from only organic ingredients. Poochie will love them." Riley's gaze flitted from the woman in the designer short set in front of her booth to Maisie. She winked.

After accepting payment for a package of bone-shaped biscuits, Riley turned to Evelyn and Maisie with a smile. "What can I do for you today?"

"We're wondering if you know anyone who'd like a cat."

"*You're* wondering," Maisie mumbled.

"We seem to have been adopted by a stray." Evelyn rested her hand on her daughter's shoulder. "Our landlord hasn't fixed Maisie's screen, and this cat keeps coming in every time we open the window, jumping in from the nearby tree. Anyway, I might consider keeping it, but our apartment building doesn't allow pets."

"Are you sure it doesn't belong to anyone?"

"We put up posters around the neighborhood a few days ago, but no one has claimed it. Plus, it's pretty scrawny. I don't think it had eaten for a while."

"Tiger's fur is soft and she lets me pet her." Maisie's voice sounded pleading as she looked up at Riley. As though the other woman had the power to change their lease.

"Aw, poor thing. Sounds like she's been starved for love as well."

Evelyn's lips tightened into a thin line. "We hoped you'd know what we could do with this cat. We can't keep it, and it's too hot to leave our windows closed. Besides, I'm pretty sure Maisie would let it in anyway."

Maisie sucked in her bottom lip as she poked the toe of her sandal against the edge of the booth.

If that wasn't silent agreement, Evelyn hadn't met it before. "Do you know someone who needs a barn cat?"

"Tiger doesn't want to live on a farm and chase mice." Maisie shot her a disgusted look. "I told you. She likes petting and purrs. She wants a person to love her."

Evelyn raised her eyebrows toward Riley in an unspoken plea. *See what I'm dealing with here?*

"Can you keep her for a few more days while I ask around? Now if Tiger were a puppy, it would be easier. I haven't done as much with cats, but there must be someone who wants her."

"*I* want her, but Mom says..."

Riley touched Maisie's arm. "I understand, honey, but there are lots of rentals where pets aren't an option. If where you live is one of them, and your mom signed an agreement, she's made a promise to obey that rule."

"We just need a different place, like a house, where we can keep Tiger *and* get a dog."

Evelyn sighed. "In a world where money grew on trees, this wouldn't be a problem." She pulled a folded piece of paper from her purse and handed it to Riley. "Here's one of Maisie's posters with a picture of the cat and my phone number."

"Aw, look at her. She's so cute."

"She's soft, and she doesn't have fleas. Mom thought she would. And she doesn't eat much."

"Thanks for the picture. It will help while I try to find Tiger a new home." Riley reached under her table. "Here's a toy for her. My treat. I don't have any cat food samples or I'd give you some to help out."

The small furry ball jingled as Riley dropped it in Maisie's hand. Whose side was the vendor on, anyway?

"Thanks." Maisie shot her mom a triumphant look. "She'll like that."

Riley smoothed out the poster on the counter. "I'll do what I can."

"I appreciate it." Evelyn would appreciate it more if the woman could take the cat off their hands today, but it made sense there was a process. Hopefully it wouldn't take long. Tiger wasn't really any trouble. With the window open, it went outside to do its business. In between, it curled up in a tight ball on the foot of Maisie's bed.

If only... Ben. Why hadn't she thought to ask Ben? She'd never seen a cat around his place. That meant he either didn't like them or just hadn't gotten around to getting one.

Evelyn looked down at her daughter's head as they wandered to the next booth, where a woman displayed pint jars with assorted jams and jellies. Strawberry-rhubarb sounded good. Maybe Maisie would like that on her toast.

Maybe her mother was feeling guilty.

Ben swung up on Halim's back. If this wasn't a good idea, it was too late. He would've liked to take Evelyn riding at least once without Maisie before this jaunt — not so much for the privacy, though there was that, but so he felt confident at least one of them knew what they were doing. Not that either Penny or Rapunzel were likely to bolt with an inexperienced rider on their backs.

He was worrying too much. It was just that Corinna had been raised riding, and it had been because of her horses that Max and Fran had helped them buy this acreage. The pony had been their gift for Zoey's third birthday.

Maisie on Rapunzel led the way down the trail along the creek bank.

Why hadn't Corinna's parents offered to sell the pony after the accident? Maybe Fran had forgotten about the purchase. It wasn't as though they ever came out to the house.

Evelyn followed the smaller pair on Penny. She sat tall and straight, nervousness emanating from her shoulders. This had definitely not been her idea.

When the trail widened, Ben nudged Halim alongside Penny. "How's it going?"

Penny's ears twitched and Evelyn glanced over. "Good. I think. It feels so high up."

"She's steady."

"I hope so." She cast him a small smile.

"I know you're doing this for Maisie. You made her day. Her weekend, maybe."

"Maybe her whole summer. But Maisie's not why I'm on this horse."

Halim tossed his head, wanting a good run out of this outing. Ben glanced at Evelyn as he leaned and patted the gelding's cheek. "Oh?"

"If it were just Maisie, I'd find a way to send her to that day camp. Cameron offered to pay for it, even."

Ben tried to find it in his heart to be jealous of hearing the other man's name but couldn't. He doubted Evelyn kissed the other guy like she kissed him. But on the other hand, why hadn't *he* thought of day camp for Maisie? "Where's that? Bigby Farm?"

"That sounds right. They do all kinds of things there, not just riding. It's the most amazing place ever to hear Evan and Oliver talk about the week they spent. There's crafts and games and stuff. And, yes, horses. Lots of riding."

"So... if you didn't ride today for Maisie's sake...?"

A smile played at the corners of her mouth. "Need you ask?"

"I think I do."

The expressions that flitted across her face fascinated

him. The gold flecks in her brown eyes danced. "No guesses?"

Ben pressed a hand across his chest. "Could it be because of me? Or maybe you felt sorry for three horses that never seem to get out of the paddock." He grinned. "Or maybe you've always had a secret desire to race the Kentucky Derby, and this is the first step."

She tossed back her head and laughed, the merry sound dissolving the last cold, dark places in his soul. "You're close. I was thinking more of bronc riding in a rodeo."

"Wow. I had no idea."

Rapunzel wandered around an outcropping of volcanic rock up ahead, disappearing from view. Maisie was safe with the pony. Ben edged the gelding so close his thigh brushed Evelyn's. He reached to touch her hand where it rested on the horn. "Whatever your reason, thank you. It means a lot to me."

Halim danced away, and Ben's hand trailed down Evelyn's arm until he clasped her fingers for a brief instant. One problem with a horseback riding date was that it didn't lend well to snuggling and kissing. That hadn't been such a big deal with Corinna. They'd flirted and played while riding then gone back to the house and — well, he'd been married to her.

Was marriage in his future again? Ever since the other evening when Darla had asked when the wedding was, he hadn't been able to dislodge the vision of Evelyn strolling toward him in a white dress carrying flowers. It didn't matter where, but it did matter when. The sooner the better.

Evelyn seemed quieter than usual but then, maybe he

was, too. Her excuse might be riding astride for the first time in her life. Her knees clenched Penny's sides and her eyes focused on the point between the mare's ears. It seemed as though she feared the slightest shift in balance would send her toppling to the ground, her feet caught in the stirrups while the horse fled.

How important was it to him that she rode? It had been a vital part of his relationship with Corinna, but Evelyn wasn't the same woman. Not at all.

Maybe he should sell the horses.

That might be okay with Evelyn, but Maisie wouldn't forgive him. Besides, he genuinely loved riding, and just because she hadn't done it before didn't mean Evelyn would hate it. Not everyone was born to it.

It had been long enough since his wife had died that Ben didn't see Corinna every time he looked at Evelyn. He wasn't tasting Corinna when they kissed. He wasn't whispering sweet nothings in Corinna's ear.

His wife was gone.

Evelyn was here. A different woman in every way, but she had captured his heart and imagination. She felt the same about him. Didn't she? Or did she see Corinna in places he didn't?

Ben glanced over. She looked so serious. So focused. "Penny for your thoughts."

"That's an entire giant horse."

He chuckled. "She's pretty small, as horses go. Under fifteen hands."

"A cat."

"A cat? Not what I expected to hear." Ben twisted in his

saddle to look at her.

"You know Maisie is obsessed with animals. You also know our building isn't very secure. This orange cat has taken to wandering in and out when Maisie's window is open the past few days. We put up posters around the neighborhood, but no one has claimed it."

"I bet she's in seventh heaven."

Evelyn sighed. "Pretty much. And I've become Jadis, the White Witch, for insisting we find another home for the creature."

"Riley—"

"Talked to her at the market this morning. She said she'd ask around, but that dogs are easier to place."

"Meanwhile, Maisie is getting more attached," he guessed.

"She sure is." Evelyn heaved a deep sigh. "I could be forgiven for forbidding hypothetical animals from moving in, but now I'm trying to kick a scrawny little thing to the curb. A known quantity. I'm a heartless fiend."

"So you need a knight in shining armor to sweep in and make her dreams come true."

She glanced over beneath her long lashes. "Whose dreams?"

"Maisie's. Or perhaps the cat's." This wasn't the moment to talk about his own dreams. Ones he hoped she shared. What they had was still new. Still fragile. Just because his heart and mind had leaped the gap didn't mean any of them were ready for the next phase.

Evelyn in a white dress. Guests. Flowers. Rings.

Vows.

He'd taken those vows before. *'Til death do us part.* And death had separated him and Corinna. The vows he'd made that day as a young man of barely twenty had been fulfilled. He'd loved and cherished her in the best ways he knew for as long as they had.

Ben shook his head, dislodging the thoughts. Evelyn wanted to talk about a stray cat, not weddings. "Why not bring the cat out here?"

She twisted toward him in the saddle. A look of horror crossed her face as her weight shifted. Ben reached to steady her, her arm warm beneath his fingers, as the mare sidestepped.

"You're okay. Penny's steady like a rock."

"Sorry. I'm not used to this. I shouldn't have moved so quickly."

"She won't let you fall." He caught Evelyn's chin and looked into her wide brown eyes. "*I* won't let you fall. You're safe with me." It seemed a bold promise, but not as bold as the ones he wanted to make. Time. They just needed more time.

"Did you say you'd take the cat?"

"Sure, why not?" Ben kept his voice light.

"But Gypsy... I thought dogs and cats..."

"Some of them don't get along, it's true. But most learn to if they live in the same household. Sometimes they even turn into best friends. Why don't we give it a try?"

Chapter 14

A KNOCK SOUNDED at the door on Saturday morning.

Evelyn grimaced. Someone must have left the apartment building's front door propped open again. So much for the security of buzzing people in. She peered through the peephole but didn't recognize the woman on the other side. When the person turned slightly, the top of a floral bouquet came into view.

Her heart skipped a beat. Ben had sent her flowers! Wow, she hadn't realized he'd think of something like that. Or that a large bouquet was in the budget of someone who managed a charity. She shook her head as she slid back the door chain. Obviously there was money somewhere. Look where he lived.

The young woman smiled at Evelyn around a massive bouquet of bright daisies and asters. "Maisie Felton?"

What? Evelyn took a step back. "M-Maisie?"

The woman looked at the card. "Yes, that's what it says. Is that you?"

"Uh, no. My daughter." Evelyn had never received flowers in her life. Not even a bunch from the grocery store she hadn't purchased herself, and this arrangement was a far cry from a handful of fake-looking mini mums. She blinked back an unexpected tear as she turned. "Maisie? Someone here for you."

"Coming!" Topped with bedhead and clad in baby doll jammies, Maisie rounded the doorway of her room. Her eyes grew wide, and her hand clamped over her mouth. Then she shrieked and began jumping up and down. "For me? Really?"

Evelyn pasted on a smile. "That's what she says."

Maisie crept closer, eyes shining, then reached a tentative hand toward the greenery. "It's beautiful."

The woman pushed the arrangement a little closer. "Here you go."

It all looked too heavy for Maisie, so Evelyn took it from the delivery woman. "Thank you." Was she supposed to offer a tip? Sign something? How would she even know?

"Have a great day." The woman turned away.

It *was* heavy. The whole mass was set in a Grecian-style urn.

Maisie shut the door before following Evelyn to the kitchen table. "Someone sent me flowers?" she asked in wonder.

Evelyn plucked the card from its little holder and handed it to her daughter.

"It's from Joanna and Grady." Maisie's voice was barely above a whisper. "It says Happy Birthday."

Grady's family owned the Akers Garden Center and attached flower shop, Blossoms by the Akers. That, at least, explained the size of the arrangement. But, while it was very thoughtful, Maisie was only turning eleven. How could a child that age begin to appreciate the magnitude of the gesture?

Her daughter dropped to a chair, plunked her elbows on the table, and rested her chin in her hands as her eyes soaked in the beauty.

Okay, so maybe Maisie appreciated it. But that didn't stop the desire in Evelyn's heart to feel special. That was silly. There were dozens of ways — hundreds, maybe thousands of ways — a man could make a woman feel like royalty. Didn't the look on Ben's face, the security she felt in his arms, the tenderness with which he kissed her, tell her the same thing?

But the flowers. Wow.

A knock sounded at the door. Evelyn stared at it for a long moment, gritting her teeth. She really didn't feel like talking to anyone right now. If anything, she wanted to crawl back in bed and yank the covers over her head. Wasn't that what Saturday mornings were supposed to be like? Not full of visitors.

Not full of flowers for her daughter.

Evelyn crossed the space and peered through the peephole to see Joanna and Kenia with big grins on their faces. Also here for Maisie, no doubt. She reattached that smile from somewhere and opened the door.

Kenia swooped in and squished Evelyn, peering past her. "Is the birthday girl up?"

"In the kitchen." Although the birthday wasn't until Tuesday.

Kenia scurried past her, leaving Evelyn staring at Joanna.
"Hi."

"Is she excited?" Joanna's eyes twinkled.

Now where had Evelyn put that smile? "She is."

"Oh, good. And it's only just begun." She gave Evelyn a conspiratorial wink. "You're not allowed to spoil our fun. I know how you feel about a big birthday celebration for her, but your daughter is special to so many of us. I still can hardly believe what she accomplished almost singlehandedly."

Because Evelyn had done nothing at all to keep the Grace Greenhouses operating? She supposed the whole thing was Maisie's idea, and her kid hadn't let the dream fade. She was still as involved as she'd been five months before. Evelyn needed to be proud of Maisie. She *was* proud of her. How could she be jealous of the attention?

"What do you mean by big celebration?"

Joanna grinned. "You're not allowed to say no. There are a lot of people in on this, okay? It's a thank you gift as much as a birthday gift."

"You're scaring me." What could be so big that it would require this conversation?

"I'm not trying to. Come on, let's find the birthday girl. I have something for her." Joanna linked arms with Evelyn and towed her into the kitchen, where Maisie sat with a box set of *The Chronicles of Narnia* amid shredded giftwrap.

"She was telling me all about how it was always winter but never Christmas in Narnia." Kenia's pleased eyes found Evelyn's. "She said you were getting them from the library and reading them together, so I wanted to give her the complete set."

"I love these stories. Aslan is so cool, and I love Lucy."

Kenia hugged Maisie. "We all love Lucy. I hope you and your mom enjoy reading the rest of the series together."

"We will." Maisie held the box toward Evelyn. "See? They're so pretty, and all the covers match."

So far so good. "What a thoughtful gift." Evelyn turned the set over and smiled at Kenia. "Thank you."

"Grady and I have a gift for you, too." Joanna handed Maisie an envelope. "Actually it is from more people. The church board pitched in, and so did Granddad."

Maisie looked at her, confused, then pulled the flap off the envelope. She pulled out a birthday card, and a piece of paper drifted to the table. Maisie picked it up. "What's this?"

"Read it." Joanna's smile took in daughter and mother.

Evelyn held her breath.

"Really?" Maisie squealed. "I can go to Bigby Farm for a whole week? Every single day?"

"You shouldn't have." Evelyn turned to Joanna.

"We wanted to. I know how much she loves horses and has begged to go to day camp."

It felt like control had slipped right out of Evelyn's hands and was crashing to a cement pad five stories down. Parenting wasn't about control. She knew that. *Knew* it. But other people shouldn't give her daughter things she couldn't.

Maisie launched at Joanna and hugged her tightly. "Thank you. Wow. This is my dream come true. And the flowers are so pretty."

"I remember how much you like flowers."

Since when? How had Joanna seen this desire when she — the child's mother — had no clue? The day camp... well, no one who'd ever spent five minutes in Maisie's company could claim no knowledge of this not-so-secret desire.

Felipe stood on the porch, brown envelope in hand. "I took a chance you'd be home."

Ben grinned. "You're welcome anytime. You know that, right? Come on in. I was scrambling some eggs."

"A little late for breakfast?"

"I went for a long ride this morning. I had some things to work through." Like his in-laws' conflicting reaction to the thought of him remarrying.

Felipe stepped into the house, his face unusually serious.

"What's that?" Ben pointed his spatula at the envelope before turning back to the stove. He heard the stool scrape over the tiles as his friend sat down, and then the rustling of paper.

Felipe cleared his throat. "I found your mother."

The spatula clattered to the floor as Ben pivoted. "You what?"

"She's remarried, plus she's shortened her first name. You had no way to know you weren't looking for Teresa Kujak but Teri Blackstone."

"Where is she? Is she doing okay?"

Felipe pointed at the stove. "You might want to turn that off."

Ben's appetite had fled. He snapped off the element and slid the scramble onto a plate. "You really found her. You're sure."

"Absolutely certain, my friend." Felipe pulled papers out of the envelope and slid them across the island. "The birthdate matches, as does her maiden name. Plus, I found a photo."

A middle-aged woman laughed as she looked up into the eyes of a gray-haired man who looked like he adored her. Ben had never seen her so joyful, but the basic face matched his memory. He picked up the photo. How could she be this happy when she'd left her family behind? How *dare* she be happy? His throat closed up. "Looks like her."

"She remarried about ten years ago and moved to Tennessee." Felipe's voice filled with sympathy. "Her husband's name is George. He's a pastor."

Ben gave his head a little shake. He sank onto the other stool as he drank in the photo. Why hadn't she contacted him? His mother was the one who'd abandoned him. She'd taken Bryanna along but sent her back to Dad a few weeks later. Did his sister know their mom was remarried? Did Dad?

And happy. That was the kicker.

"Her contact information is on here." Felipe tapped the other paper.

Ben's eyes tracked over. Took in the list of bare details. There was really no doubt. That had to be his mom. At the bottom was an email address and a phone number.

"That's George's number at the church. I wasn't sure... I thought you might prefer to go that route. Talk to him first."

"She looks happy."

"She does."

"How is that even possible? To meet some guy on the

internet, decide you're in love, take your kid — leaving your other one behind — and go meet him? Find out he's a triple-timing jerk?" Ben shoved the photo away. "And then be happy."

Corinna had tried so hard to find his mom, convinced she was a drug addict or worse on a street corner in Birmingham. This passion had fueled her zeal for homeless people. She'd seen Teresa Kujak — or whatever her name was now — in every homeless woman. In every dejected face.

"It's been fifteen years."

"She's the one who ruined all our lives. My father is an alcoholic. My sister has trouble trusting men. I'd be nothing if Corinna hadn't loved me, and I still ended up alone."

"Your father was an alcoholic before your mother left, Ben. You told me he always drank too much. They didn't have a good marriage."

"But she's the one who walked out."

"I'm not excusing her. You serve the homeless. The needy. You must believe they deserve better or you wouldn't bother. Many of them made specific decisions that landed them where they are now. Others were pushed aside or marginalized for various reasons. Wouldn't you be happy if the people you serve found their way back into society as functioning members?" Felipe nudged the photo back toward him. "Found happiness again? Found hope in a Savior?"

Of course that's what he wanted for them. It had even happened to a few.

Guilt smote him. It had happened to Evelyn. She'd been on the street. She'd gone into soup kitchens and homeless shelters clutching a small child by the hand. She'd found a mentor who'd given her compassion and training, and look at her now.

Irony piled upon irony.

"When's the last time you spoke with your dad?" Felipe asked quietly.

Ben shook his head, trying to dislodge the newly aroused emotions. "Not long after the funeral."

"Five years. He still lives in Twin Falls, my friend. He's still your father."

"You and Constance come from big happy families. No one disreputable?"

"Every family has one or two. That great-aunt who belittles everyone. The uncle who tells bawdy jokes in front of the children."

Ben folded the paper around the photo and shoved both inside the envelope. "I don't know what to do with this." Hadn't he said for years he wanted to find his mother?

"I suggest praying." Felipe rose and leaned on the island. "Maybe talk to your sister."

Bryanna had moved back to Arcadia Valley a few months ago. Last he'd heard, she was working for Grady's family at Blossoms by the Akers. Somehow Ben rarely thought to connect with his sister.

"And talk to Evelyn. Let her be part of your solution."

Maybe Corinna's family was right. Maybe his time with the charity should come to a close. Maybe he didn't have it in him anymore.

Chapter 15

"CHANGE OF PLANS, SWEETIE."

Maisie's jaw tensed as she glowered at Evelyn. "But I want to go to Ben's and see Tiger and Gypsy and Rapunzel."

"I know you do, but I want to do something special for your birthday. I didn't know we couldn't do it on Tuesday, but now that you're going to day camp—" the thought still burned "—today's the only day."

"Tiger needs me. Remember Ben couldn't find her the other day because she was hiding. Gypsy scares her. I want them to be friends."

"You'll have lots of chances to see Tiger." Ben hadn't been in on this scheme to give Maisie her heart's desire, had he? No. Evelyn was pretty sure not. "C'mon, get ready. You've always begged to go out to see the Craters of the Moon National Monument."

"I guess." Maisie took a long, lingering look at the massive bouquet.

"When we get home, we'll get take-out from El Corazon

and start reading the third Narnia book. How does that sound?"

Maisie sighed. "Okay."

Evelyn watched her daughter walk to her room. She'd be eleven on Tuesday. Surely that was too young for this amount of attitude. Evelyn grimaced. Not that she wasn't showing some herself. If eleven was too young, twenty-eight was too old.

She marched into her own room to get ready for the day. *Please, Lord, let Maisie and me have a good day together. My little girl is growing up. She has a heart of compassion, and I pray that tender side will keep growing. And help my attitude, please? Help me to be grateful for everything I do have and to enjoy Maisie's flowers without jealousy.*

A while later they were on the highway heading northeast with a praise CD cranked in the car. The impromptu prayer session had lifted Evelyn's spirits, and Maisie was singing along to her favorite songs.

The town of Shoshone was in the rearview mirror when Evelyn's cellphone rang. She glanced at it in the console. Ben. She should've called and told him her plans. Not that they'd specifically made any, but she and Maisie had spent the past few Saturdays at his place.

"Want me to answer?" asked Maisie.

"I've got it." Evelyn tapped the brakes and angled to the highway's shoulder as she turned down the music. She picked up the phone. "Hi there."

"Hey, beautiful. What are you up to today? How about a picnic?"

"I'm sorry. That sounds lovely, but Maisie and I are on the way to the Craters of the Moon."

"Oh. I always enjoyed visiting there when I was a kid."

She should've invited him along. What had she been thinking? Right. About how he hadn't ever given her flowers. But was that worth snubbing him for? It wasn't that he'd done anything wrong. Far from it, really.

"We've never been before." Having a local guide was another reason she should have asked him, but it was too late. They were nearly halfway to the monument. "It's Maisie's birthday on Tuesday, and this was my chance to have a special day with her."

He chuckled.

Did it sound forced? She really should have called.

"When's school back in?"

"This is her last full week of vacation, and Joanna and Grady and some others paid for a week at Bigby Farm for her birthday, so that fills most of it."

"She'll enjoy that."

Evelyn sighed. "She really will." She'd taken charity for so many years it shouldn't bother her to accept a big gift like this, but the flowers had already set her on edge.

"All right then. Can I pick you up for church in the morning? Maybe we can make a day of it."

"I'd like that. Maisie is worried about Tiger."

"The cat is fine. Tomorrow's a plan then. I've had some news about my mother I wanted to share with you, but it can wait until tomorrow."

Suddenly she wished she hadn't started out on this trip today. Maisie was barely interested. Evelyn wanted nothing more than to be at Ben's, wrapped in his arms as he bared his soul.

"Have a great day with Maisie. Talk to you later."

Evelyn lowered the cell to the console and reached for the gearshift.

"When can I see Tiger?"

"Tomorrow after church." She glanced over her shoulder and angled the car back onto the highway.

"Are you going to marry Ben?"

Evelyn gripped the steering wheel and focused on the gray ribbon of road stretching between fields of sagebrush. To her left in the distance, the Sawtooth National Forest barely smudged the horizon with its hills. A semi-truck carrying huge bales of hay headed southwest, probably on its way to deliver feed to one of the many dairy farms near Arcadia Valley.

"Mom?"

"I don't know, sweetie."

"You kiss him and hug him. You hold his hand."

And he gave her a sense of security like she'd never felt in her life before. "Yes, those things are true."

Maisie spread her hands, palms up, and raised her eyebrows. The unspoken *duh*.

"It's too early to be certain everything will work out that way."

"It's sad that his little girl died. She might've been my friend."

Did Ben see Zoey every time he looked at Maisie? His daughter would have been a couple of years younger. Hopefully the connection wasn't constant in his mind.

Evelyn was pretty sure he didn't think of Corinna every time he kissed her, because that would be beyond weird. In a world where Zoey lived while her mother died, the girls might have known each other. "She might've."

Maisie flopped back against the seat. "Anyway, I like Ben."

"You sure it's not just Gypsy and Rapunzel you like?" Evelyn couldn't help teasing.

"I like them, too, of course. I like his house and that it's not so hot inside all the time. I like the creek, and that the swimming hole is only a few minutes away. And I like that he took my cat home with him, even if Tiger is afraid of Gypsy."

"They'll work it out."

"What do you like about Ben?"

Evelyn glanced over at her daughter. "I like that he loves Jesus and cares about people who need help." *And how he kisses. And how he makes me feel cherished.*

"Do you think he's cute?"

In her mind's eye, Ben grinned at her, his shock of brown hair mussed from her hands running through it, his brown eyes glinting in amusement. Oh, yeah, he was cute all right. "Mmhmm."

"So if you married him, we'd move to his house, right? Tiger could sleep in my room again. She misses me. And Ben would be my dad. I bet he misses having a daughter."

"Sweetie, don't get your hopes up too much." A sermon she should be preaching at herself, too. "It's a big decision, and it takes a lot of time and prayer to make sure it's the right one."

What would she say if Ben asked her? It would take her half a second to say yes, throw herself in his arms, and kiss him like she meant it. He wouldn't even need to give her flowers.

Her heart already knew. Did his?

"So. Tell me about your mother." Evelyn gave him a sidelong look.

Ben pushed out a smile. "That sounds so Sigmund Freud."

"I wondered if you'd catch the reference."

"When you used that tone of voice? Totally." He tossed a small piece of lava rock into the creek, well downstream from where Maisie and Gypsy played.

Evelyn studied him. "Did you hear from your mom directly?"

He shook his head, not meeting her gaze. "Felipe and I got talking a couple of weeks ago, and he offered to do a basic search. With his connections, it didn't take long to track her down."

"So where is she? Is she okay?"

"She's remarried. Felipe found a photo of her online. She seems happy." He chucked a larger rock into the stream.

"That's good. Right?"

"I think so." He glanced at Evelyn. "I know it seems petty to wish she'd suffered more, but the hurting kid she left behind is having a hard time letting go."

Evelyn slid her arm across his shoulder. "I get that. I can't bear to think of Buck as a happily-married respectable member of his community."

He leaned into her comfort. "Have you looked him up? Found him on Facebook?"

"No. I don't want to know."

"Not even a little?"

She shook her head. "If he ever cared what happened to his daughter, he could find out. I haven't changed my name or tried to hide."

Was that what his mother had done? Tried to hide?

"Why do you think your mom never contacted you? Are you going to ask her?"

"I haven't decided." The piece of paper with the contact info burned in his pocket. "Like you, I haven't hidden, either. I'm living within twenty miles of where she left me. What kind of mother purposefully walks out of her child's life and never looks back? How can she be happy now?"

"Fifteen years is a long time. Maybe she hasn't been in a place where she felt she could reach out. She probably feels very guilty."

"Sure doesn't show on her face." He knew he sounded sulky, but what was a guy supposed to do with a wound this deep? One where the scab had been pulled off to reveal nothing had been healed beneath it? Maybe it was a good thing Evelyn and Maisie had gone to the badlands yesterday. He'd been considerably more morose then.

"Ben." Evelyn's fingers massaged his shoulder. "Have you talked to God about this? Asked Him to help you forgive her?"

He shrugged, but it didn't dislodge her hand. "I've tried. Believe me. It's ironic. Corinna tried so hard to find my mother. It's what led to her passion for homeless people. The reason her parents started the charity after she died."

"How come your friend could find her when Corinna couldn't?"

"He's connected with private investigators through the police force. Maybe Corinna didn't try to get help. I don't remember. Or maybe my mother has surfaced more recently."

"That could be. Things have opened up a lot online in the past few years."

"This has me questioning everything I'm doing with my life. Everything's in turmoil."

Her fingers drifted down his back and away.

Ben caught her hands. "I didn't mean you. You're the one bright spot. I don't know what I'd do without you."

She bit her lip as she watched Maisie stack a monument of rocks in the creek.

"Evelyn, please." He wrapped his arm around her, tugging her close. "The kind of turmoil you've brought into my life is the best kind. You make me feel alive. Like good things can happen after years of mere existence."

"I'm sure there are people who don't think I deserve happiness. Some days I am one of them."

Ben shook his head. "But who could..."

Her finger pressed to his lips. "I made some big mistakes, Ben. Different ones than your mom made. I hurt some people deeply, too, but Jesus is bigger. He taught us love. Forgiveness." She looked into his eyes. "Compassion."

155

"I don't know if I have it in me to manage the charity anymore." Was he in the wrong?

"I don't understand. Think about Fred. Rona. The others. What will happen if you close down the soup kitchen?"

Ben looked away. "The family will find someone else to run it. I'm not sure if it's a good fit for me.

"Because of your mother?"

"Partly. I don't know. It feels like it's all built on a farce. She didn't need help."

"But you weren't doing it for her. Not directly." In his peripheral vision, he could see her studying him. "You said partly. What other reason?"

This was way harder than he'd thought. Why had everything happened at the same time instead of single file? "I mentioned to Corinna's family that I was seeing someone. I felt... they should know."

Evelyn nodded slowly. "And?"

"Her mother ran out of the room crying, and her dad said they needed some time to think before we talked again."

"Oh. I'm sorry." She shifted away from him on the rock.

"I used to work in construction. I could probably get a job again. Drew Harrison might be hiring, or there are others."

"I don't want to come between you and Corinna's family."

"Evelyn." He pressed a kiss to her temple. "Corinna is my past. You are my present. I-I hope you're my future. I love you."

The universe paused, silent. He hadn't meant to say those words. Not yet. Not now.

That didn't mean they weren't true. It just meant the timing was off. Why didn't she answer? Was she unsure of his feelings? Of her own? Or had his poor-me confession turned her away?

"I-I care for you, too."

His heart plummeted. Not love?

"It's too soon," she went on. "There's too much going on for me to think straight."

"Sometimes our hearts know." His had with Corinna. It did again now.

"You have some big decisions to make. I can't make them for you. I can't influence you in them."

Sure she could. Whatever she said, he'd go and do. Stay at the charity? Great. Resign and find a job in construction? Perfect.

Forgive his mother? Harder, but he'd try. He really would.

Evelyn clambered to her feet. "I think it's time Maisie and I headed for home. I'll be praying for you, Ben. Praying for wisdom."

He opened his mouth. Shut it again. That was all she had? No words of love and commitment in reply to his? No promise to be at his side no matter what he was going through?

Disappointment knifed through him. Guilt. Fear. "I'll give you a ride home."

Chapter 16

THE GREENHOUSE GARDENS exploded with ripeness. Volunteers prepared mega-batches of pasta sauce to freeze into large tubs for Corinna's Cupboard. Mrs. Marshall offered a chest freezer her family no longer needed. Over all, Evelyn couldn't have been more satisfied with how the project had turned out.

Today was Maisie's birthday but, since she was at day camp anyway, Evelyn joined the group in the church kitchen. The place hummed with activity as several chatting women chopped onions, peppers, and herbs. The aroma of simmering sauce filled the air.

Evelyn dipped another load of ripe tomatoes into boiling water, poking at the peels, and waited for them to crack.

Beside her, Joanna slipped the skins off the previous batch, now submerged in cold water, and angled a glance at her. "Why so quiet?"

"I've never done this before. I don't want to mess it up."

Joanna plopped another peeled, cored tomato into a large bowl on the other side, where another woman diced it into small pieces. "I've never done it before, either. My parents didn't garden, and they certainly didn't preserve food for winter."

Evelyn lifted the loaded strainer from the boiling pot.

Joanna shifted out of the way as the tomatoes tumbled into the ice water. "Did you learn to cook at home?"

Was that some kind of joke? There'd been cans and packages in the pantry along with personal-size cheese-and-cracker packs. She'd chosen what she wanted to eat when she was hungry and heated it herself if needed. "Nope. I picked up a bit here and there over the years. It's just since we moved to Arcadia Valley and I've been able to support Maisie and myself that I've focused on cooking. On nutrition."

Her friend swiped a loose hair off her face with her forearm. "You never talk about your parents."

"It's a door I'd rather keep shut, thanks."

"Yet you think Ben should forgive his mom?"

Evelyn chomped down on her bottom lip. In the background, a pot clanked onto the other stovetop. Sautéing garlic and onions permeated the air. Smothered in the rich tomato sauce, the aroma was half a step short of heaven.

"It's a different situation."

"I see a lot of similarities. While one pair pushed their teenager out the door, the other mother walked away from her teen without a word. The results were the same. Broken, abandoned kids."

Abandoned. Yes, that summed it up. "True. Psalm 68:5 and 6 have been a rock to me in that regard. 'A father to the fatherless, a defender of widows, is God in his holy dwelling. God sets the lonely in families...' It carries on from there, but that's the gist."

"God's also in the healing business," Joanna mused. "Sometimes the restoration comes full circle."

Evelyn stabbed a sharp blade into a tomato that bobbed at the top of the boiling water. Cracks spread from the cut and surrounded the orb. "Incoming." She dumped the load into Joanna's sink and turned to fill the strainer with more round, red fruit. "You see the cracks on those skins?"

Joanna held up a tomato, her blade poised against a curling edge. "Yes?"

"Sometimes there's no restoration. Sometimes the old skin has to go so the fruit can be made into something new. Something better."

"Sometimes analogies break down." Joanna chuckled as she removed the peel. "Although even here, these are headed for the compost, where they'll decompose and add to the soil's nutrition for next year's garden."

"Nothing is wasted. So true."

Joanna glanced around the kitchen then leaned closer to Evelyn. "Do you pray for your parents?" Her knife excised a bad spot from the tomato she'd just peeled.

Her words probed, too, exposing an ugly wound.

"I don't think you can be too hard on Ben if you can't do the same thing yourself. It's like pointing out the speck in someone else's eye when you have a plank in your own."

"It's completely different."

"I don't think it is." Joanna's voice was quiet.

Evelyn had looked up her parents' address a year or two ago. They still lived in the house she'd once called home. Why had she even spent two minutes on the internet search if she hadn't thought of contacting them? She'd closed the browser tab, curiosity abated for the moment. But she hadn't forgotten. She imagined them doing the same things they'd done every day. Dad reading the paper, too absorbed in the stock market to wish her a good day at school. Mom too busy with her job as a mall manager, her garden club — roses, not tomatoes — her hundred and one other important activities.

Had there even been a hole in their life when she left? Had they noticed beyond no longer needing to stock the snacks she'd preferred? She'd been fatherless — motherless — well before that night behind the bleachers. Abandoned. Unloved. No wonder she'd been so quick to take a tumble with the quarterback.

"Evelyn?"

She turned to her best friend, aware of the tears puddling in her eyes, and raised her eyebrows. No smile, no words, were anywhere to be summoned.

"Write them a letter? Include a copy of that photo of you and Maisie where you look so happy with each other? Give them your email address. Your phone number. Give them a chance to respond and make amends."

Like she'd told Ben, she doubted she was that hard to find online if someone spent a few minutes looking. If she could find them, they could find her. But, while she'd been little more than a child when they'd pointed at the door, she was an adult now. A woman who, despite all odds, had been saved by grace and landed on her feet far from home.

Ben's pain from his mother's betrayal was so clear to her. Were her issues as visible to him? Was she hiding her pain only from herself? *Lord, forgive me.*

Ben pulled in at Bigby Farm at the end of the day and parked beside Felipe's van. His buddy's face lit up. "Are you here to pick up Maisie?"

"I am." Joanna had phoned him to ask if he'd do the honors. She and Evelyn's pasta-sauce making day at the church kitchen was dragging longer than expected. That was all the permission he'd needed, even if it wasn't direct from Evelyn.

Two of the younger Espinoza girls darted toward Felipe. He squatted and gathered them in his arms as they chattered and showed off little lavender-stuffed pillows. "Where's Kaleena?" he asked, when he could get a word in edgewise.

The five-year-old pointed toward the barn. "She and Maisie found baby kittens. They're so tiny their eyes are still shut."

Ben nodded to Felipe, grinning. "I'll go find them."

The farm spread out before him. Children dashed toward incoming vehicles, waving their pillows.

A woman came out of the barn as Ben neared. She angled a glance at him. "I don't believe we've met. I'm Caroline Hearst."

"Ben Kujak." He stretched out his hand and shook hers. "Here to pick up Maisie Felton. I understand there are kittens in the barn, which would explain why she didn't come out to meet me."

Caroline chuckled. "Sounds like Maisie. Let me check if you're on the list. Can I see your ID?"

He pulled out his wallet. "Joanna Kraus told me my name was there. She's the one who paid for Maisie's week. I'm Maisie's mom's... boyfriend." What a weird word.

"The children's safety is my primary concern. I'll be back in a minute." She narrowed her gaze at him. "Don't leave before I return."

"Fine." He shrugged. "Which way to the kittens?"

Caroline didn't answer, just brushed past him on her way to the house.

Ben shook his head and entered the barn, his eyes taking a few seconds to adjust to the dimly lit interior. "Maisie?"

"Ben!" Maisie's head popped over the edge of the loft above his head. "There are kittens. Come see."

"So I heard." He climbed the ladder and made his way across the loose hay.

"Shh." Maisie put her finger to her mouth.

Kaleena looked up at him, eyes shining. "Look, aren't they the tiniest things ever?"

Five little balls of sleek fur in assorted colors squirmed beside a gray cat, who lay on her side, engorged teats pointing at her offspring. She didn't seem all that concerned about her audience.

"Her name is Smoky," whispered Maisie, touching the cat's head. "They're so sweet. Do you think Tiger will have babies?"

"Maybe." He hadn't taken time to determine if the feline was male or female, so he went along with Maisie's belief. The orange cat always wanted back outside after she'd eaten.

"I want lots of cats. And dogs. Dozens of them."

"That's a lot." Just the thought made Ben a little weak, though a couple of more of each kind couldn't hurt.

Kaleena stroked a black kitten with white paws. "I want this one."

163

"This bunch will need to stay with their mama for a long time yet." Ben rose. "Your dad's waiting for you, Kaleena. And I'm here for you." He nudged Maisie's shoulder.

"Mom said they were cooking boatloads of pasta sauce for Corinna's Cupboard today." Maisie patted each kitten on the head before standing. "They're still busy?"

He nodded. "Sounded like it. Come on." He followed the girls down the ladder, and they ran ahead of him toward the waiting vehicles.

Caroline came toward him, clipboard in hand. "Please sign her out."

"I've passed muster?"

"Your name was on file. You understand that the children are under our care. Who knows when someone's ex will visit unannounced. We can't let just anyone take the children."

He thought of Buck randomly showing up to kidnap Maisie. "I understand. You can't be too careful. I get it." He nodded at her as he scrawled his name. "Have a great evening."

"You, too."

Ben could only hope. Now he needed to swing by the church kitchen and see if Evelyn would let him take them out for dinner. It was Maisie's birthday, after all, and their friends had plans.

She was a mess. Her pink T-shirt was splattered with tomato sauce, and her hair had partially unraveled from the bun she'd contained it in this morning. Evelyn hadn't even worn makeup for this kitchen day.

In front of her, in the church kitchen doorway, a beaming Maisie clung to Ben's hand and jabbered endlessly about kittens.

Ben. Unlike her, he looked put together even this late in the day in khaki shorts and a black muscle shirt. Hair combed. Gelled, even. More than put together, he looked... hot. In the amazingly sexy way, not because the temperature outside was still pushing one hundred in the shade.

"Hi. I didn't expect to see you." Pretty obvious, no doubt. Her eyes focused on his while her hands tried to fix her hair, but it was no use. Nothing but a shower, a hairbrush, a change of clothes, and some time with her makeup had the power to improve her appearance.

A grin crinkled the skin around his eyes. "Thank you, everyone. I can't believe you're doing all this for the soup kitchen." He gestured into the room behind her, where several women, including Joanna, finished the last few dishes and wiped counters.

"You're welcome." The thought that he might leave the charity — for her — didn't sit well. Ugh. What a mess the past few days had been. And, thanks to Joanna, Evelyn felt edgier than ever faced with her daughter's hand in Ben's.

"I'd like to take you and your birthday girl out for dinner. A little bird told me you didn't have big plans."

Thanks, Joanna. Her hand strayed back to her hair. "We can't. I'm a mess."

Maisie's shoulders drooped.

165

"It's early yet. Only quarter after five. There's time for you to shower and change if you wish."

What did she wish? That she'd had a loving family, that she'd told Buck no, that Ben's mom hadn't deserted him, that his dad wasn't an alcoholic... it was a long list. Wishing didn't change anything. Praying helped, but it didn't undo the past.

Maisie peered up at her through lowered lashes.

Her daughter deserved better. All those things weren't her fault. While they'd had their moments, as had any parent with a girl headed into puberty, Maisie was normally upbeat and caring. And she obviously wanted Ben included at her birthday celebration.

Evelyn took a deep breath. "Okay. Where do you want to meet? Is six all right?"

"How about The Jukebox? I know it's not super upscale, but Maisie said something about wanting a hot dog. How about if I give you and Maisie a ride home? I can wait at your place, and we can walk together from there. It's just a few blocks."

He acted like he hadn't rocked her world two days ago. Declaring his love. Refusing to forgive his mother.

Joanna had reminded Evelyn she was no better. Could they deal with their past hurts?

How would she know if they didn't keep trying?

Chapter 17

BEN PULLED THE DOOR to The Jukebox open, gesturing for Maisie and Evelyn to precede him. He rested his hand on the small of Evelyn's back as they entered the fifties' style diner. *Great Balls of Fire* by Jerry Lee Lewis blasted past them into the street then stopped in mid-beat.

"Surprise!" The single word exploded from dozens of smiling faces. "Happy birthday!"

Ben rammed into Maisie when her feet welded to the black-and-white tiled floor half a step in front of him. She whirled and crashed into his chest. He steadied her.

"For me?" She looked up into his face, eyes wide and shining.

"Happy birthday, kiddo. Enjoy." He might have been speaking to Maisie, but his arm had slid all the way around the child's mother, who stood beside him still as a statue.

167

Maisie dashed toward Kaleena. There must've been fifty people gathered, many of the garden volunteers as well as a few Ben didn't recognize, all wishing her well.

"You did this?" Evelyn asked quietly from beside him. She turned into the circle of his arm.

He suspected it was more to keep the conversation private than anything else, but he'd take it. "Blame Joanna and Kenia."

"I wasn't prepared. She and I had her birthday dinner at El Corazon on Saturday. I thought she'd be tired from a long day at camp, and we'd have a quiet movie tonight at home."

Ben looped both arms around Evelyn's waist as he had done so many times before. She didn't melt against him, and he doubted the reason was the public place. Something had shifted on Sunday. Something had come between them. Could it all be blamed on his reluctance to contact his mother? "You thought a day of riding and playing would tire her out? Really? That kid's a total extrovert. She thrives on activity and people."

"Unlike her mother."

"You're one of a kind, and so is she."

"At least they're not all staring at me."

The crowd closed in around Maisie. It seemed everyone wanted a piece of her. A few, like Joanna, sent questioning glances toward the door. He and Evelyn still blocked it. Several waitresses in poodle skirts and saddle shoes set clinking glasses full of ice cubes and water around tables arranged down the side of the café.

Ben rubbed his hands on Evelyn's back. If only she leaned into him. "Come on. Time to find a seat."

"Ben. Was this your idea?"

"Not completely. I ran into Joanna a few days ago, and she said we should have a party for Maisie's birthday, and I agreed. She came up with this." He longed to cradle her face between his hands. To kiss her. But she still stood like an unbending reed. "I hope you're not angry."

"Did you see those flowers in the apartment?"

He nodded. "They're very pretty." Ben couldn't have missed them. For a panicked moment he'd thought Cameron or some other man might be wooing Evelyn, but a glance at the card while she was in the shower proved otherwise. Why hadn't he ever thought of having a bouquet delivered? It might mean talking to his sister, but he should do that, anyway.

"From Grady and Joanna. Also the week at day camp. Now this?"

Ben turned Evelyn so she faced the group. He kept his arms around her and leaned close to her ear. "Look who's here." He'd avoid mentioning Cameron and the twins. "Everyone is paying for their own food, except I invited you and Maisie, so I'm picking up your tab. The Jukebox supplied the balloons and streamers and will serve the cake afterward. Grady's parents ordered that from Demi's Delights."

"I'm overreacting," she whispered. She pushed free of his arms and strolled toward the tables. Kenia hurried over and hugged her.

What he wanted to know was why Evelyn was unnerved, but this wasn't the time for probing questions. Likely she'd turn the tables and counter with a request for him to contact his mother. He could wait for that discussion for years.

And yet… there was no way he could keep avoiding the packet of information about his mother and keep Evelyn in his life. She wouldn't allow it. It had already come between them. Was the pain of going back into his murky teen years and dealing with his feelings worth it? Was there anything his mom could say to help him heal? How about his dad? Because once Ben had dived in, he had to swim to the other side.

He didn't want to.

Evelyn linked arms with Kenia and rounded the end of the pushed-together tables.

Even now, if he wanted to sit next to her, he needed to move. Ben closed the space and held a chair for Evelyn. She smiled at him, a wary look still lurking in her eyes, as she sat.

The buzz of conversation simmered as several dozen people found seats and opened menus. Some from the church. Some greenhouse volunteers. Many friends.

Ben slid his arm across the back of Evelyn's chair and leaned close, inhaling the clean scent of her shampoo. "Know what you want to order?"

Further down the table, Cameron's gaze caught on Ben's for a few seconds. Something shone there. Jealousy? Regret, maybe.

If Ben refused to reach out to his parents, would Evelyn turn to Joanna's brother?

"Mom! Mom! The screen in my window has been fixed."

Evelyn pushed out a tired smile. "That's great. The

building manager must have come in while we were at The Jukebox." Would've been nice if he'd let her know in advance instead of just showing up while they were gone. Weren't there laws about that? Not that she'd have turned him away, of course.

Now if only she could afford a window A/C unit. Maybe next summer. Even now, the nights were starting to cool down to something bearable. Just a few more weeks and the seemingly interminable heat wave would be broken.

Maisie padded out of her room wearing her favorite baby doll jammies a few minutes later. She snuggled up beside Evelyn on the sofa. "This has been my best birthday ever."

"I'm glad, sweetie." The funk Evelyn found herself in wasn't her daughter's fault. If anyone deserved to be spoiled, it was Maisie. She'd worked so hard on the greenhouse project it shouldn't be surprising that people wanted to offer recognition for it.

"I got those beautiful flowers, and a whole week at day camp, and then that fun party." Maisie sighed in contentment.

"And..." Evelyn nudged her.

"And a day at Craters of the Moon and supper at El Corazon. Thanks, Mom."

"You're welcome. I wish I could do more, that all those other gifts didn't have to be from other people."

Maisie looked up at her, brows pulling together. "It's okay. Last year on my birthday we had a picnic at the swimming hole. Remember? And you got me my bike."

A second-hand bike. "I remember."

"That was pretty cool, too." Her daughter's head rested on Evelyn's shoulder.

How much longer would Maisie be her little girl? She was already so big. So independent. Such a force to be reckoned with. "I love you, sweetie, and I'm very proud of you."

"I'm proud of you, too."

"Me?" Evelyn blinked. "For what?"

"You're a really good mom. I mean, I wish I had a dad, too, like my friends, but I think I have the best mom in Arcadia Valley."

"Aw, thanks, sweetie."

Maisie's head angled to look up. "What happened to my dad? And how come I don't have any grandparents? Kaleena has some, plus dozens of cousins and aunts and uncles."

They'd had a basic birds-and-bees talk a long time ago, but this was the first time Maisie seemed interested in her heritage. Evelyn gathered Maisie tighter against her side. "I made a big mistake when I was a teenager, and I had sex with a guy I didn't even like all that much. Remember I told you how babies happen? Well, that's when you started to grow inside me."

Maisie's eyes widened and her lip curled.

"My mom and dad were very angry with me and told me I couldn't live at their house anymore. Even though they are your grandparents, that's why you don't know them."

"That's not very nice."

"No, I agree. Your dad didn't want anything to do with me or you, either." How would Maisie feel about all the rejection in her young life? "His mom and dad — your other grandparents — helped us for a while. But then they died when you were two."

Maisie scowled, and assorted emotions raced across her face. "Can I write a letter to my grandparents? Maybe they'd like me now if they had a chance."

"Maybe." Was Evelyn ready to open that door? "We'll see. Want to bring *The Voyage of the Dawn Treader* over here? We can start reading it tonight."

Maisie crossed her arms and looked up at Evelyn. "You always say we'll see when you don't want to do something, and you hope I'll forget. I won't forget."

Busted.

Evelyn pushed a smile to her face. "I'll think about it. I promise. Want to go get the book?"

Ben's sister opened her door at his knock. "Hey, big brother. What brings you here?"

"I know it's late, but I needed to talk to you."

Bryanna grinned. "Nine-thirty isn't that late. Come on in. Can I get you a drink?"

He shook his head as he followed her into her apartment. This was a much nicer building than Evelyn's, plus the management kept it maintained. He wondered when Evelyn and Maisie would discover the fixed screen? He'd slipped it in place while Maisie was in the shower and Evelyn was in her bedroom getting ready for dinner at The Jukebox.

Bryanna curled up at one end of her sofa. "So, what's up?"

She had a right to wonder. Of all the people in his family, she was at least as much a victim as he was. Why hadn't he done more to keep in touch, especially since she'd moved back? She must feel as abandoned as he did. Ben wedged his elbows on his knees and leaned forward in a chair. "Have you kept in touch with Mom?"

"Would you hate me if I said yes?"

Ben rubbed his hands through his hair. "I'm trying to understand."

"Dad was pretty hard to live with. I'm sure you remember that."

There was no room for denial. He nodded.

"I'm not saying Mom went about things the right way, because she didn't. But I don't blame her for leaving Dad."

"But she deserted us at the same time. Well, me at least. She took you with her."

"That didn't last long." Bryanna grimaced. "The guy in Birmingham was a pimp."

Ben reared back. "A *what*?"

"You heard me. He wanted Mom to go to work for him. Wanted me, too. When Mom caught him making advances on me, we were out of there in no time flat. That's when she called Dad."

"But... I never knew this."

"You never asked, and I didn't want to talk about it."

Ben ran his hands through his hair. "She remarried."

"I know."

He surged to his feet and paced the small room. "You knew? Why didn't you tell me?"

"You haven't exactly made communication easy." Bryanna drew her knees up under her chin.

"No. No, I haven't. I'm sorry." He stared out the window

into the dusk. "I just don't understand why she's never contacted me."

"Were you in any place to accept it?"

Ben pivoted. "It doesn't matter. She gave birth to me. How could she simply abandon me and never look back?" Apparently his sister was special. That burned.

"Dad made her promise before he sent the plane ticket for me. Promise to leave us all alone and never contact us."

"But... how do you know this stuff? Why didn't you tell me?"

"Ben, I wasn't in a good place, either. When I got home, you were so distant. Closed off. Then I went away for college, and I never heard from you. What was I supposed to do?"

He'd been a terrible big brother.

"I was there in Alabama. It was hard for Mom. She knew she'd messed up, and her back was against the wall. She didn't feel she had any other choices but to accept Dad's ultimatum."

"But you've been in touch." Ben heard the accusation in his voice. How could Bryanna have kept this from him?

"Not until I was an adult living on my own. You were married to Corinna. Happy. I didn't want to mess up your life. And then when she and Zoey died, it didn't seem a good time, either. You pushed everyone away, Ben."

He had. He knew he had.

Chapter 18

"HOW IS IT SO DIFFERENT?" Joanna studied Evelyn's face.

"It feels different."

"You want Ben to reach out to his mom and forgive her, but you're not willing to do the same thing for your parents?"

Put that way, there were definite similarities, but it wasn't exactly the same. "My parents kicked me out."

"While Ben's mother left physically, and his dad left emotionally. Both of you were abandoned when you most needed support and guidance."

"Don't forget love."

Joanna angled her head. "Yes, and love. The very people who brought you into this world rejected you. That has to hurt deeply. I see the same thing in Evan and Oliver, even though they were not quite four when Lisa left."

"Stop trying to set me up with Cameron."

"I'm not." Joanna covered Evelyn's hand with her own. "Right now you're in turmoil over Ben. If, in a year or two, you're over him and healed, I'll mention my brother again.

But I think you and Ben have possibilities, and I hate to see you pulling back instead of trying to work through them."

Evelyn glared at her friend. "Who said I wasn't trying? I don't even know what to do here."

"Maisie wants to contact her grandparents. That seems a reasonable request."

"They'll reject her. They rejected me."

"It's been twelve years, Evelyn. They may have a heap of regret."

"If they did, they could have found me."

Joanna poured another cup of tea for each of them and nudged the honey jar closer to Evelyn. "Are your parents believers?"

Evelyn narrowed her gaze at her friend. "They weren't when I was a kid, that's for sure."

"And Jesus has offered you forgiveness and a new hope. Don't you think your parents deserve to hear about it?"

She clamped her teeth shut and glared at her friend. There was no easy way out of this conversation. Joanna wouldn't accept no for an answer. If the shoe were on the other foot, Evelyn wouldn't, either.

"This thing with both your parents has come between you and Ben. Isn't it worth doing whatever you can to reconcile with the past so you can move forward?"

"But he should..."

"Maybe he needs you to be an example."

Evelyn surged to her feet. "I'm tired of being the strong one. The one who struggles to do the right thing."

"Hon, happiness is within your reach, but you're pulling back. Why?"

Evelyn crossed her arms, leaned back against Joanna's sink cupboard, and glared at her friend.

"You're afraid."

"You're stretching for motives."

"I don't think I am." Joanna studied her. "There's no other reason I can think of why you'd hold back. You're afraid your parents will reject you again. What can they do to you that they haven't already done?"

"Maisie."

Joanna shook her head. "Pardon me? You're afraid they'd take her from you? They can't."

"No, not that." Although, emotionally, Maisie *was* a target. Wouldn't she be thrilled to have doting grandparents?

"Then what?"

"It would crush her to be ignored or pushed away. I can't do that to her."

"It wouldn't be you doing it. Besides, she's a tough kid. Resilient. And she wants a relationship with her grandparents. Can you blame her?"

Sighing, Evelyn shook her head. "No, I can't."

"Then... reach out." Joanna's words were soft. "Don't cradle the hurt any longer. Don't let this stand between you and Ben." She held up her hand. "I know it's not the only thing. I know he has some forgiveness to do of his own, but reaching out to your parents will put the ball squarely in his court. It will show him you're serious about making things work with him."

Evelyn's eyebrows rose. "How do you get all of that from a letter or phone call?"

"What would it tell you if he said he'd tried to make

things right with *his* parents?"

That she mattered enough to him to do hard things for. "Yeah, yeah. I get it." She didn't have to like it, but she got it. She sighed. "It's possible — likely, even — that I'd go to all that effort, baring my insecurities, and Ben and I still won't work out."

"Two things there. One, you'd have a new sense of peace about your parents. You'd know that you went back to them as an adult and gave them another chance to know you and Maisie. You can't tell me that won't positively affect you every day for the rest of your life."

Evelyn inclined her head. "And the second thing?"

"I'm not sure why you're so pessimistic about Ben. Just a couple of weeks ago, he was the best thing ever and you were giddy about the possibilities."

"He's moody."

"And you're not?"

"Hey!" She pushed away from the cupboard. "How did this become pick-on-Evelyn day?"

Joanna grinned. "You came to me for a shoulder to cry on."

"Obviously a mistake."

"I don't think so. What kind of friend would I be if I didn't give you some gentle love?"

"You call that gentle? It felt more like a swift kick in the butt."

"Love does that when needed. Tell me you haven't done it to Maisie."

"That's different. She's my child."

Joanna rose and met Evelyn halfway across the small

kitchen. "Yes, but it's love. When you love someone, you say the hard things because you care about them." Joanna enfolded her in a hug. "And I care about you. A lot."

Evelyn tried to resist the hug but couldn't. She wrapped her arms around Joanna. "Thanks. And you're right. I'm terrified. I never planned to open this door."

"I'll pray for you. Listen, what are your hours like next week? I'd like to take a girls' day to Boise and look at dresses for the wedding. Is there a day that works for you?"

"Next week is bad." Evelyn grimaced. "I've got month-end billing for Dr. Winchester. At the very best, I'll be putting in a couple of evenings at home."

"The week after?"

"That would be better. Sounds fun."

"Hey, Evelyn." Was this where Ben said he hadn't been sure she'd show up at the soup kitchen, even though Friday afternoon was her scheduled volunteer time?

She gave him a small smile. "Hi."

He reached one hand toward her. She stepped closer, and he slid his arms around her. "I've missed you," he whispered into her hair.

"I've missed you, too." But she didn't lean into him or tip her face for a kiss. "Sorry. It's been a rough week."

Ben slid his hands up her back. "I'm sorry to hear that." He'd had a rough one himself, especially his visit with Bryanna Tuesday night after Maisie's party. "Anything you want to talk about?"

Evelyn's fingers clenched a fistful of his T-shirt then smoothed it as she shook her head. "What do you need me to do today?"

Kiss him? Tell him everything would be okay? How could he fight for her if she blocked him out? "It's roast night. Normally I'd ask you to peel potatoes."

"But I brought you a big bucket of baby potatoes. They'd take forever to peel."

"I know. Scrub them? They should be okay with gravy even if they're not mashed, right?"

"They'll be perfect." Still she stayed in the circle of his arms. "What else are we preparing?"

"A salad? And I thought we could do a wok full of those green beans the way you made them at my house on Sunday." It seemed like a lifetime ago.

Evelyn nodded and pushed away, but Ben wasn't ready to let her go. He pressed his lips to hers. She kissed him back without the passion they'd shared recently then stepped out of his grasp. Her smile didn't reach her eyes.

Had he scared her so much by telling her he loved her? It couldn't just be that.

She dumped the bucket of earthy potatoes into the deep sink and turned on the tap. A minute later the swish and ping of scrubbed orbs landed in the large saucepan.

Ben sharpened a paring knife then began cutting the tips and tails off the green beans. "How has Maisie liked her week at Bigby Farm?"

"Good. Between all the horseback riding and the newborn kittens, it couldn't have been much better."

"That's great." Man, they'd lost a lot of ground. Even the

first time or two they met, they'd had more than this to say to each other. "I talked to my sister the other night."

That got her attention. Evelyn paused with a potato in one hand and the brush in the other. "Oh?"

"Bryanna's been in touch with our mother for years."

"And she never told you?"

"We're not exactly close." Ben nipped the end off another bean. "To think I could have just asked her and saved Felipe the hassle."

"Ben, I'm sorry. That must hurt."

It had stung like crazy, actually. Still did. "Bryanna said it was part of the deal Dad made with Mom. He'd take my sister back, but Mom had to promise never to contact us."

"Then..."

"Bryanna looked for her a few years ago. Found her."

"You said you have her email and her phone number. Are you going to reach out to her?"

This was the pivotal moment. Ben stared across the small space at Evelyn, and she stared back. "Yeah. I think I am. I'm just not sure what to say. 'Hey, remember me? The son you gave birth to?'" He shook his head. "I probably need to find a way to rephrase that."

"It's a big step."

She'd know, if anyone did. "It's been a long time coming. I feel a little better, knowing Dad made her promise to leave us alone."

Evelyn sucked in her lips and turned back to the potatoes.

Right. Her parents didn't have such a handy excuse. They'd just up and kicked her out when she needed them the most.

"Evelyn? I'm trying to do what I can. I didn't see it before last week, but now I understand how my anger about my mom was affecting everything in my life. I want to love you with a pure heart, not as someone holding onto bitterness."

"That's great for you." She swallowed hard.

Push her to talk? Give her space? Before he could decide, she went on.

"Joanna asked me to be her maid of honor. Sometime soon she wants to spend the day in Boise looking at dresses." Evelyn darted a glance at him.

Corinna and her mom had spent an unbelievable amount of time and money on her dress. On the entire wedding. In his mind's eye, Corinna, with her hand tucked at Max's elbow, strolled toward Ben down the red runner in the church, her face beaming and her eyes twinkling. He'd stood and waited for her, hands clammy and pulse jumping.

He and Corinna had been two kids playing house. There hadn't been anything wrong with that. She'd meant everything to him. Everything.

But he loved Evelyn with a more mature love. Sure, life had knocked him around some as a teen. The situation with his mom had hit him hard. He'd taken it out on his dad, and it sounded like that hadn't been misplaced. But it was time — past time — to make amends as an adult. He couldn't fix the past. There might not be a great relationship in the future. But it couldn't be his fault. Not if he wanted to come to Evelyn, ready to love her with a healed and whole heart. And he did.

"...green or blue. I'm not sure which."

Ben blinked. "Pardon me?"

"The colors for the wedding."

"The... wedding?"

"Joanna and Grady's? That's what I've been talking about."

"Oh. I guess I zoned out."

"Men."

"Hey, what's that supposed to mean?"

"Men don't care about weddings. They think the whole thing is overblown."

"Evelyn?" He waited until she glanced over at him. "Guys definitely care about weddings. At least their own."

The flush on her cheeks as she renewed scrubbing potatoes gave him hope.

Chapter 19

THE OUTSIDE DOORS of the greenhouse creaked open. Evelyn stretched as she turned from her desk. Her gaze landed on a Latino man with graying hair. Not one of the volunteers, although he looked vaguely familiar.

She rose and extended her hand. "Hi, I don't believe we've met. I'm Evelyn Felton."

"Max Martinez." His handshake was firm. Almost too firm.

It clicked. His face and name were on several real estate billboards around Twin Falls. But why was a real estate agent at the greenhouse project? The living trust had given Grace Fellowship the legal deed for the property. Surely someone would have let her know if anything had changed.

"Pleased to meet you. What can I do for you, Mr. Martinez?"

His dark eyes pierced hers. "Tell me about what's going on here." His hands spread.

"Th-the greenhouse project?"

He nodded, but had yet to smile.

How far back did she go? "This property was the original

location for the Akers Garden Center. When Barry Akers took over from his father twenty-five or so years ago, he moved the business and expanded it. Eventually, as his father aged, this property was completely decommissioned. In the last year, the old man entered full time care at Retro Village and turned the property over to Grace Fellowship in a living trust." The man in front of her was a real estate agent. She wouldn't have to explain how that worked, would she?

At her questioning look, Max nodded, obviously waiting for her to continue.

"Elderly Mr. Akers wanted the property used for something that would benefit the community and help those who needed it most. The decision was to invite volunteers to grow food for the local soup kitchen." She smiled brightly.

"Did Corinna's Cupboard ask for assistance?"

Why would an agent from Twin Falls know the name of Arcadia Valley's resource? She took a closer look at the man, but his impassive face gave her no answers. "No, sir, they didn't. In fact, it took a while to figure out how best to utilize the fresh produce, but I think we all have a good system in place now."

"The original system was working."

Evelyn took a step backward at the intensity in the man's face. Who was he, really? He didn't seem to be here under the guise of real estate. "I beg your pardon?"

"There was enough food. Enough resources. Interference was unnecessary."

Oh, hey, now. One of *those*? "I don't think there are ever enough resources to help those in need, and fresh, healthy produce is a huge improvement over canned and packaged food past its expiry date."

"Those in need." He shook his head, but the glitter didn't leave his eyes. "Many of them deserve everything that's happened to them."

Evelyn raised her chin. "That is completely untrue. Do you think anyone would stand at a crossroads and purposefully choose the direction that leads to homelessness and hunger? I know I didn't."

His eyebrows shot up. "Pardon me?"

Gah, she hadn't meant to say that, but this man riled her as few had since she'd gotten off the streets. "I've lived it. I know my own story and can tell you how dozens of other people found themselves without a job, without a home. They're real people, Mr. Martinez. Real people who once had dreams and a spring in their step. Doesn't everyone deserve hope?"

He glared at her as though he could dissect her with his eyes.

She stepped closer. "I think they do, sir. I was sixteen years old when my parents kicked me out because I found myself pregnant. Can you say that one choice — to have sex with the quarterback behind the bleachers — was made knowing it would render me homeless for nine years? In that one hormone-flooded moment, I made what seemed a small choice. I didn't expect the repercussions. None of them."

"I'll grant there could be occasional situations like that, but you have to admit there's often a pattern. It usually takes more than one poor choice."

"And sometimes it is someone else's choice. My daughter lived on the streets of Memphis with me for almost half of her life. None of it was her fault. She was created in God's image just as you and I were, Mr. Martinez. Do you have any idea how painful it was to be unable to meet a single one of her needs without accepting charity from strangers? Many of whom, like you, cast judgment as to whether or not we *deserved* it?"

His arms crossed as he widened his stance and opened his mouth to speak.

She didn't want to hear a thing this pompous man had to say. "Mr. Martinez, I now work three part-time jobs to provide a home and basic necessities for my child. Most of the people I knew on the streets of Memphis would consider our story a huge success. But why me? Why not them? I had a mentor. A woman who stepped in beside me and continues to do the same with others. She helped me finish college. She paid for daycare for Maisie. She taught me the value I have in Jesus. And that is why I helped Maisie spearhead this project for Corinna's Cupboard. To give back. To give hope."

His eyes narrowed. "Your *child* initiated this?"

"She did." Evelyn smiled proudly. "She was only ten and a half years old at the time, and she already had compassion for those in need." *More than you do, sir.*

"That probably explains why this didn't go through the proper channels."

"I beg your pardon? I didn't know there were rules for helping others. We have about fifty volunteers who make things happen around here. Some gardening, some processing, and some cooking over at the soup kitchen."

Max Martinez shook his head. "Of course there are channels. Corinna's Cupboard is a registered charity run by a private foundation of which I am chair."

Evelyn felt her mouth gape but felt powerless to close it. How could he be involved and still believe the worst of all the people his charity helped?

"Corinna was my daughter, Ms. Felton. Don't try to tell me I don't know how a charity like this should operate. It's been running for five years in my daughter's name, and it's been running just fine without interference."

Evelyn's brain scrambled to catch up. This man was Ben's father-in-law? His employer? What all had she said, anyway? Had she said anything that would jeopardize Ben's job?

She could just see reaching out, shaking his hand again, and saying something like, 'great to meet you. I'm in love with your daughter's husband.' Yeah, that'd go over really well, no matter how long Corinna had been gone.

"The board consists of my wife and I and our remaining children. We feel this situation has gone on long enough. We have the funding to pay Ben Kujak's salary and operate the charity as we have been doing. Do you?"

Emailing would be safer. Ben could write out all his thoughts and feelings and censor them before they ever reached his mother. No, he hated writing. The other option was phoning his mother's husband. His stepfather.

Ben looked at the photo of the two together for the hundredth time. What could he tell from the picture? That for at least one moment in time, his mother had been happy, smiling into the eyes of someone who loved her back. Someone who was not Ben's father.

He couldn't remember his parents ever having a moment like that. Instead, there had been a decline from tolerance to constant bickering and drinking. Had they ever actually loved each other? They must've, or why would they have married in the first place?

But that era was well and truly over, fourteen years back. Half his life ago.

George was a pastor in a church in Memphis. That made him a good guy, right? Plus, it was still business hours back east. Ben grabbed his phone and punched in the number as quickly as he could, before his nerve ran out.

"Hi, this is George."

Ben swallowed hard. "George Blackstone? My name is Ben Kujak."

"Ben! Wow, it's so good to hear your voice. I've heard so much about you."

"I, uh... you have?"

The man chuckled. "Maybe I should ask the reason for your call."

"I understand you're married to my mother, Teresa."

"I am. She's a wonderful woman, Ben. You'd be so impressed by the person she's become."

"She left me. I was just a kid. I needed her."

"And you felt betrayed. I understand."

How could this man understand? Ben took a deep shuddering breath.

George went on. "I'm sure as an adult you realize it was your father she was leaving, not you."

"My head knows that I was collateral damage. My heart... just knows the damage."

"Ben, when a family fractures, the loss is felt by every member, even though it's rarely a rejection of the kids. Your mother prays for you every day. Longs to hear from you."

"But I'm not the one who ran away. I'm right here where she left me. How hard could it have been to find my number and call me?"

"She'd made a promise to your father."

Ben laughed, the sound harsh and cynical to his own ears. "She also promised to love him until death parted them. She had no problem breaking that one."

"I'm not a proponent of divorce. I need you to know that your parents' marriage was over years before I met your mom. She'd already become a Christian... Ben, are you a man of faith? Do you believe God's word?"

Ben clutched the small phone tightly. "I am. My wife introduced me to Jesus."

"I understand she's passed on, along with your young daughter. Please accept my sympathy. Teri and I were crushed at the news. We have prayed and prayed for you."

"Wouldn't that have been a good time to contact me?" He sounded like the bitter fourteen-year-old he'd once been. "I could have used a mother about then."

There was a slight hesitation. "I'm sure you could have, son. Believe me, it has been a difficult promise for your mother to keep. Your sister reached out a few years ago, so Teri has heard a bit of your news from time to time."

That hardly seemed fair. Ben was still angry with Bryanna for never telling him. Not that he'd gone out of his way to offer support to his sister. No, he'd been involved in his own world and ignored hers. He'd felt rejected then passed the emotion on to others, never getting too involved. Sure, he prepared meals for Rona, Fred, and the others, but he hadn't poured himself into their lives. He'd thought the distance was grief from Corinna's passing. Now he wondered if it wasn't the rejection he'd suffered as a young teen.

"I'm sorry, sir. I'm still really struggling with all this. A police officer friend of mine used his resources to locate my mother. When I told Bryanna, I learned she'd known for years. She was the child Mom took with her when she left. Now, once again, Bryanna had inside knowledge, but not me. Kicked in the teeth all over again."

"I'm very sorry."

What difference did it make? It hadn't changed anything. Well, apparently it had for his mother. Nice for her. Ben took a long breath and pinched the bridge of his nose. *Lord, I'm spiraling here. Please help. Bitterness and anger have been part of my life for far too long. I need it to go away. I don't want to feed it.*

"It's all been rather a lot of shock. I'm not sure how I expected my mother's story to end, but to find she's married again — and to a minister, no less — was definitely not how I thought it would go down."

"May I tell you about her?"

"Please."

"When she put your sister on the plane in Birmingham, she was at the end of herself. She'd gambled on the man she met online only to find out he was worse than your father. He was a drunk, but this man was involved in the sex trade."

"Bryanna said he was a pimp."

"Yes, basically. Anyway, there she was. Alone. Far from Idaho and the only home she'd ever known. Yes, she was free of your father, but she'd also cut ties with her two children. She'd made some poor decisions, and she was paying for them."

Did he even want to feel sympathy for the woman his mother had been? But there were always two sides. Hadn't Evelyn shown him that?

"She walked into a church on a street corner in Birmingham, all the way to the front, and collapsed at the foot of the cross. She was at the end of herself. The church secretary found her there, sobbing, and led her to Jesus."

Ben could see it in his mind. The broken woman. Had he really wanted her to stay shattered for fourteen years? Of course, he hadn't.

"I'd like to say that was the day everything changed for her, but it wasn't. Not externally, at least. It took several more years of struggling to keep a roof over her head and a decent job. When I met her about five years later, she'd just been transferred to Memphis and was already mentoring other women who needed a helping hand, picking up where she'd left off in Birmingham. She's an amazing woman, Ben. I need you to know that I love her very much. I'm so thankful for her genuine, generous heart."

His mom was a success story, not someone who stayed in the system forever. One of the ones who gave back, like Evelyn's mentor. Ben closed his eyes, asking God to wash away fourteen years of bitterness.

"Many women she's worked with have re-entered the

workforce and gone on to have stable homes and families. Some of them have moved across the country and landed on their feet." George chuckled. "One of them, a single mom whose parents kicked her out when she got pregnant as a teen, even ended up in your part of Idaho."

Ben's gut froze as the pieces snapped together with a near audible click. If he'd been standing, he'd have been in danger of toppling over. "I'm sorry, sir. I need to go now." Without waiting for a reply, he stabbed the end button.

He could imagine the man at the other end looking at his phone in confusion, but there was no way he could keep making small talk with his mother's husband.

Not when Mom had been Evelyn's mentor.

Chapter 20

VELYN STOMPED AROUND the greenhouse with short, jerky steps.

Had that man *threatened* her?

Her mind filled in all the things he hadn't said, but he'd said enough. Basically get out of Ben's life and take her vegetables with her. Things had already been awkward with Ben since the other day. Now?

"Evelyn? You here somewhere?" Joanna called.

"In here." Man, she needed to get her voice under control. It wouldn't do to show her vulnerability to her best friend. One of the few friends she had at all.

"There you are." Joanna's shoes crunched on the gravel. "I was sure I'd catch you here waiting for Maisie to finish school for the day."

Evelyn turned and smiled. It felt more like a grimace.

Joanna stopped a few feet away and tilted her head. "What's wrong?"

"Nothing." But she was going to have to tell Joanna sooner or later. This wasn't something she could quietly do on her own.

Her friend's eyebrows rose.

"Okay, not nothing. I'm just not ready to talk about it yet."

"Uh oh." Joanna hopped onto the nearest planting table then sat with her legs swinging. "Let me guess. Ben did something male and stupid."

Like fall in love with somebody who might have a diploma in business admin but still didn't know to jump through all the hoops in the right order. "Not Ben. Not directly."

"Then why don't you want to talk about it? Because by now, I'm sure I'm imagining something worse than what could have happened."

"I doubt it." Evelyn rubbed her eyes and shook her head. "You know Corinna's Cupboard is named for Ben's wife, right?" She managed to get the words out without choking on them. Maybe she could do this.

"Yes."

"So her family, her parents, run the foundation. I don't know, do fundraisers, whatever. They pay Ben's salary."

"Uh huuuh."

"Max Martinez. The real estate mogul in Twin Falls. You've seen him on a dozen billboards."

"Was that the man who left a few minutes ago? He looked vaguely familiar, and that would explain it."

"Yeah. Probably driving something swanky."

Joanna shrugged. "I don't keep up with car styles, but yeah, it looked like money. So, what did he want?"

"He wanted to know if we could run the charity without his foundation."

"He... what?"

Evelyn raised her eyebrows. Like her friend couldn't figure that out.

"Is this because of you? Because he couldn't possibly have a problem with fresh, real food."

"He only talked about food. Apparently homeless people should be grateful for whatever crumbs they get, because they brought their situation on themselves anyway. And we didn't go through *proper channels*. Which I guess means groveling before his majesty."

"Wow."

"Look, I'm sorry. I didn't want to talk about it now, not when I'm still so angry I can't see straight."

"Evelyn, I'm your friend. That means I care about you, and I've got your back. I'm glad I came down here. It felt random, but I think God nudged me to it."

Evelyn stabbed her toe at the gravel. "Thanks."

"Are you sure he wasn't here checking out Ben's girlfriend?"

"Other than making sure I knew he was Corinna's father, there didn't seem to be anything personal about it."

"But it would make more sense, wouldn't it? For him to be upset about his former son-in-law in a relationship? Why should he care if the needy people have vegetables or not? It's not taking away his personal resources. No one asked him to pay for the greenhouse."

"You think so?" He *had* seemed to know who she was.

"Pretty sure, hon. Maybe he's the kind of man who likes controlling others. If benevolently doesn't work, then a step further."

Evelyn brushed her hands together. "Fine. He wins. I'm resigning as project coordinator. The church can do what they like with the remaining produce." She'd let Buck and his lawyer uncle win once before. She was in better shape to weather the storm this time.

Joanna's mouth gaped. "You can't mean that. It's your passion."

"It was Maisie's passion. She's back in school, busy in sixth grade. I'll find another job. Waitressing or something. I've done it before and can do it again." Maybe Morgan Taylor would hire her.

"Why? Why let him win? I thought you loved Ben."

"How should I know? I don't have any experience with love. I like him a lot, but I can't be the reason he loses his job."

"Don't do anything rash. I know you two love each other."

"You don't understand. It's not just me, Joanna. It's the people who depend on Corinna's Cupboard. If the charity closes, it will be on my head."

"It won't. It will be on Max's."

"But I can prevent it."

"Please tell me you'll talk to Ben before you do anything else."

Right. The Ben who'd already said he'd be willing to get a job in construction again for her. Said he loved her. How had she responded to that? By running. Like she was running now, but it was for his own good.

She shook her head. "I don't think I can. I can't put him in that spot."

"You mean making him choose between you and the charity?"

"Ben can make a bigger difference doing what he's doing there. I-I'm used to standing on my own. I'll be okay without him." She hated that her voice shook.

"Do you really think Corinna's family would shut down everything because of you? He wasn't bluffing?"

Evelyn shuddered. "I don't want to find out. I'm not worth it, Joanna."

"That's the old Evelyn speaking. The one who lived on the streets."

"That's *me*." She jabbed her thumb at her breastbone. "I'm still that same woman. Don't you understand? Rona. Fred. The others. I'm not better than them. They have no one but Ben standing in the gap for them. I can't take that away from them. I can't do it."

"There might be another answer. Maybe Grace Fellowship *can* take over the charity. How will we know if we don't ask?"

Evelyn shook her head. "There's way too much money involved. With only a few weeks left until frost, we'll let the volunteers take home the remaining produce and call it done."

"Do you think all this—" Joanna's hand waved in a big circle "—will simply disappear because you're afraid to face up to Corinna's father?"

"I'm not afraid of him."

"Then what are you afraid of?

"Look, I—"

"No, you listen to me. Is this what you want to teach

Maisie? That when something is tough, you quit? This was her brainwave to start with, if you recall. You think she's going to let you roll over and play dead?"

Maisie.

What time was it, anyway? Her daughter had been due here after school ten minutes ago.

Ben dismounted, opened the paddock, and led Halim in. A long ride had done little to clear his head. He had no way to know if Evelyn realized her mentor was his mother. Hadn't she once said the woman had found this job for her from way over in Memphis? Maybe her mentor had also said, "Go out to Arcadia Valley and keep an eye on my son."

Maybe that's why Evelyn had spooked the other night when he'd told her he loved her. Because she didn't love him back, but was only investigating him.

But that couldn't be true. Their relationship was real. It had grown bit by bit all summer. He'd kissed her. She'd kissed him back. No way was she that good an actress.

He swung the saddle off Halim and reached for the curry comb before realizing the dog hadn't come to meet them on their return. "Gypsy!" he hollered.

A woof sounded from in the barn.

"Come on, girl. I'll get you a treat." That was a word sure to bring her running. Only it didn't. "Gypsy?"

That was weird. Ben patted Halim. "Be right back." Then he swung open the barn door and peered into the darkness. Had she gotten stuck somewhere? "Hey, girl, where are you?"

"Go!" whispered someone.

Gypsy whimpered as Ben's eyes adjusted. "Maisie? Is that you?"

Silence.

Ben narrowed the distance to where the girl lay curled up in a ball, hugging Tiger to her chest. Gypsy looked between him and Maisie, obviously torn. Ben crouched and rubbed the dog's head. "Good girl, Gypsy."

"Go away." Maisie's voice was gruff and muffled.

Ben lowered himself the rest of the way to the hay and touched Maisie's hair. "You okay, honey? What happened?" Also, did her mother know she was here? It seemed unlikely.

"My mom said she wouldn't bring me, and I missed Tiger and Gypsy."

"They missed you, too." He felt his lips curve upward. "Did your mom say why?" He hated to use a kid as a go-between, but something had to give way. If Maisie could offer a clue, it might help.

"I wrote a letter to my grandparents, and Mom won't mail it. Other kids have grandparents. Why can't I?" The girl pulled herself to sitting then scrunched the squirming cat tight against her chest.

Ben had no answer. For Zoey's few short years, she'd been doted on by Fran and Max. His own mother, of course, had rejected him and thus Zoey. No. He needed to remember the new spin on that story. He hadn't known all the pieces.

Maisie didn't, either, but he still agreed with her. Kids should have grandparents.

"What did you say in your letter?"

"I told them about the greenhouse and the gardens, and

about Tiger, and about Bigby Farm, and... well, about everything."

"Must be really long."

"Three pages! I used my notebook paper from school."

"That's impressive. So you're mad at your mom, huh?"

Maisie dashed one arm across her eyes. "Yeah."

He'd like to say Evelyn was only doing what she thought was best, but he happened to agree with her daughter. "Does she know you're here?"

The head shake was barely discernible.

"Honey, she'll be worried about you."

"She was talking to Joanna, and she sounded angry." Maisie peered over at Ben. "Mom doesn't usually get mad."

Tread carefully, Ben. "Did that make you nervous?"

"Yeah. I needed Tiger." Maisie's lip trembled. "She has such soft fur. I needed to hold her."

The bedraggled cat had filled out a bit since coming to live at the acreage.

Maisie dropped her gaze and pressed her cheek against Tiger. "And I know Gypsy's your dog, but sometimes I pretend she's mine."

"Maisie, honey..." Ben's voice caught. How could he promise anything to this child? It wasn't his decision to make. Not alone. His heart had already decided, though. Whatever it took to smooth things over with Evelyn and make the three of them into a family — along with Tiger, Gypsy, and the horses — he'd do it. He'd talk to his mother. Forgive her. See his father. Close the charity.

Anything. Whatever it took.

"What?" Maisie peered up at him.

"You're a really special kid, you know that? I have a new job for you. A project."

Her eyes brightened.

Ben grinned. That got her attention like treat did Gypsy's. "I love your mom, and I love you. I want us to be a family." He held his finger over his lips. "You can't tell her that. It's still a secret."

Maisie shrugged.

"No, I mean it. Some things have to happen, and they have to happen in the right order, and the right person has to do them. Do you understand?"

"Like I was the right person to get the volunteers, but first we needed the greenhouse and Grady's granddad."

"Kind of like that."

"So what's the project?"

"First I need to know what you think of my idea of being a family."

She tipped her head to one side. "Would we live here? With you?"

He nodded.

"Riley has this really sweet puppy. I saw him at the farmers market last weekend, and she said he needs a home."

A parade of animals marched through Ben's mind, and he couldn't help chuckling. "What does he look like?"

"He's mostly white but has cute brown spots around his eyes." Maisie lowered her chin and stared at Ben. "Mom said no."

"You know why she said that."

Maisie waved a hand. "Yeah, I know. The apartment. But if we were a family and lived here..." Her eyebrows went up.

Was the kid bargaining with him? Ben laughed and nudged her shoulder with his fist. "I'm sure we can find room for another animal or two around here. If that's what it takes to win you over."

"Thank you." She flung herself at him, nearly knocking him backwards into the hay with her exuberant hug. "So what's the project?" She settled back on her heels.

Ben rose and dusted the hay off his jeans. "I'll tell you on the way to town." He pulled his phone out of his pocket and handed it to her. "Call your mom, please. I need to give Halim a quick brush down, and we can be on our way."

Chapter 21

EVELYN PULLED THE APARTMENT DOOR open and glared at her daughter. "There you are. I was crazy worried when you didn't show up at the greenhouse after school. I was ready to dial 9-1-1."

Maisie scuffed her shoe and glanced up at Ben, who had his hand on her shoulder. "I called you."

"No, you didn't."

Maisie's jaw clenched. "I called you from Ben's phone, but you didn't answer."

Evelyn fought a boatload of emotion. She couldn't deny seeing Ben's name come up on her phone and letting it go to voicemail. She needed time to figure out how to handle Max's threats. "If I'd known it was you, sweetie, I would've answered." She didn't need to look at Ben to see the hurt on his face. She loved him. She did. Oh, so much.

A sudden thought struck her. "Why didn't you come to the greenhouse?"

"I did."

Evelyn's heart sank. What had Maisie overheard that sent her pedaling all the way out to Ben's? "I didn't see you."

"You were talking to Joanna. You sounded angry."

She didn't want to get into this in front of Ben. She didn't want to explain it to Maisie, either. The wall of solidarity in front of her pierced her to the core. Maisie would never forgive her for turning Ben away. But if Evelyn could get a job waitressing at L'Aubergine, maybe they'd still be able to get a rental house and bring Tiger home. Or maybe the landlord wouldn't notice if they snuck the cat into the apartment. No, she couldn't do that. She'd made too big a deal of being a rule-follower.

Evelyn forced herself to meet Ben's gaze and push out a smile. "Thanks for bringing her home. I'll see it doesn't happen again."

"She's welcome anytime."

Those deep brown eyes did their best to suck her in, but she looked down at Maisie. "Come. Please."

Her daughter glanced up at Ben, who nudged her forward. Maisie dashed down the hall and slammed her bedroom door.

Leaving Evelyn with a man blocking the door to the apartment. "Thanks again." She wouldn't be able to hold it together much longer. All she wanted was Ben's arms around her, his lips on hers. Why did she have to be the responsible one, carrying the destiny of so many?

"Sweetheart, we need to talk." His finger traced her jaw. "Please tell me what's going on?"

She shook her head and took a half-step back. Out of reach.

Except that he came inside and wrapped her in his arms. She grabbed a fistful of his favorite gray T-shirt and inhaled the manly smell of him before trying to push away, but his arms only tightened.

"Okay, I'll talk to you even if you won't talk to me," he said. "I called George today."

She braced herself. "Who's George?"

"My mother's husband. Did I ever tell you my mom's new name?"

"I don't think so." Her voice sounded even, right?

"Teri Blackstone. She works with homeless people in Memphis, Tennessee."

Evelyn's world spun. Would she faint dead away? "Teri? M-my mentor? Your mother?"

"You didn't know?" The roughness in Ben's voice forced her to look up at him.

"No. How could I have?"

"You said she'd found the job listing for you to apply for at the town office. She didn't say she used to live here? Had family here?"

Evelyn's head shook even as she raked her memory for hints. "No. Nothing."

She could feel the tension slip out of Ben's body. That meant she was too close to him. She should step away, but she couldn't. Not when this was likely the last time she'd be in his embrace.

"Evelyn."

Oh, the emotions her name evoked when murmured like this. By this man. Evelyn slid her hands down his arms until she could push away. "Ben, I think—"

His mouth covered hers, tasting, exploring, leaving no doubt to the depth of his emotion.

She melted against him for a brief moment, giving as well as receiving, before her brain kicked back in, holding an image of Rona at the forefront. Fred. "Ben, no."

"I love you, sweetheart. You mean the world to me. You and Maisie. I'm even fond of that orange ball of fur."

He couldn't be proposing. Not now. Not when everything was in such a turmoil. She jerked away from him and stopped a few feet away, arms wrapped around herself. "Please don't, Ben." She couldn't meet his gaze. "It wasn't meant to be."

"How can you say that? You've brought me back to life. Pushed me to reconcile with my parents. Rejuvenated the soup kitchen."

"Stop. No." Tears pushed hard, but she blinked them back.

"I don't understand. I love you. I know you love me."

She'd never said the words, but that didn't make them less true. "Sometimes love isn't enough. You have to trust me."

"I've trusted you with my heart."

And she'd offered hers back. Why did everything have to be so hard? All the time? She was no stranger to self-sacrifice. She'd given up everything for Maisie twelve years ago. It had been ongoing ever since. "Ben, I... Mrs. Marshall will be coming into the soup kitchen tomorrow instead of me."

"Won't you tell me what happened, sweetheart? We can pray together. God can fix anything."

Not this. Some problems could only be solved with a selfless act. She was no Aslan. She was more like Edmund, who'd betrayed everyone but still found a way to redemption in the end.

"Evelyn, I won't go away that easily, but I'll leave you now — for a little while — if you make me a promise."

She hated the sound of that. Tears flooded her eyes as she tried to look at him.

"Send Maisie's letter to your parents. Include a note of your own if you can. I'm so thankful you pushed me to contact my mom. Even though I'm only halfway there, it's already a blessing in my life." He hesitated, searching her face. "Sweetheart, this is super important to your daughter."

"Yes, yes. Fine."

Ben blinked. "You will?"

"Sure." Anything to get him out of her apartment. She needed space to think, and he was right. Sort of right.

"There's one more thing."

"No. You said one promise. I made it." Her voice faded to a whisper. "Please, Ben. I can't take any more."

"Don't keep Maisie from me. We need each other. All three of us. I'm leaving now, but it's not because I'm giving up. I love you, Evelyn Felton. I love you with all my heart, and we will find a way through this, whatever it is."

With a quick step forward, he clasped her in his arms and pressed a kiss to her forehead. "I'll talk to you soon." And he was gone.

How did a woman with a shattered heart write even a short letter to the parents who'd broken it in the first place? But she'd promised.

Ben pushed the buzzer beside the door to Joanna's basement suite. He'd never been here before, and he could only hope her brother wasn't watching out the upstairs window and get the wrong idea. Whatever that might be.

The door opened and Joanna blinked through her blue-framed glasses. "Ben. What a surprise."

She didn't sound in shock. "Hey, Joanna. Do you have a few minutes? Can we talk?"

"Sure. Come on in." She stepped aside. "Can I offer you coffee or tea?"

Ben shook his head as he followed her in. "No, thanks." His gaze landed on a huge bouquet of flowers on the small table in the corner, even bigger than the one Maisie had received for her birthday. Must be nice for Joanna dating a guy whose family owned a flower shop.

Uh. Other men could buy flowers, too. Corinna never cared. She said they wilted too quickly, but she was always happy to add another ring or bracelet or pair of dangly earrings to her eclectic collection. Which kind of woman was Evelyn? He didn't even know.

"Grady spoils me." Joanna glanced between him and the flowers.

"I see that." He followed her through the archway into a small sitting room half filled with a large desk with an open laptop beside neat stacks of paper. "I'm sorry. I caught you at a bad time. You were working."

She sat in the only easy chair. "No problem. Some would

say I'm a workaholic, but I'll always take time for a friend. Have a seat."

He sank onto the end of the small sofa and met her gaze. She watched. Waited. Didn't seem to be surprised by his presence. Finally he blurted out, "What went wrong with Evelyn and me?"

Joanna's eyebrows tipped above her glasses. "Tell me what you think of her."

Not the response he expected. "I love her. I never thought I would find love again after Corinna and Zoey died, but God had other plans. Or, at least I thought He did." Ben shook his head. "Things were going well. We've been getting to know each other for the past couple of months or so, spending a lot of time together. Talking. Getting past some of that initial hard stuff."

"Let me guess. She told you it was over, and it was for your own good, or something like that."

He leaned his elbows on his knees and ran both hands through his hair. "She didn't even give me that much. Joanna, I know it's not because she doesn't care. She kissed me back. She was crying, but she still sent me away."

Should he have stayed? Just sat down on her bedraggled sofa and refused to move? Half of him screamed yes. But it wasn't all about who could be more stubborn. Love didn't work that way. Love had to be a give-and-take with a foundation of mutual respect. Not one person being a bully.

"When did things go wrong?"

"A couple of weeks ago? Before Maisie's birthday, I think. She was already on edge about letting Maisie accept those gifts from you. And then I told her I loved her, and I'd

211

do anything for her..." There'd been more to the conversation, but wasn't that the most important part?

Joanna's head angled to the side. "What kind of anything?"

He laughed. "It wasn't a big deal. I'd told Corinna's parents I was seeing someone, and they were less than impressed. Sure, they operate the charity, but I can get another job if they make it difficult. I used to work in construction, and I hear Drew Harrison is hiring. I might be able to get on with him. Or there are other contractors."

"You told her?" Joanna's voice was soft. "Think about what you said."

"What do you mean?" He spread his hands. "It's a man's responsibility to provide for his family. I want to marry Evelyn. I want to be Maisie's dad. So I need an income, and if it isn't from the foundation, then elsewhere."

"Keep thinking." Joanna's brown eyes practically bored holes through his.

"I'm a guy. I need a little more help."

"What has Evelyn's life been like the last twelve years?"

"I know! How can I not want to make it better? I love her."

"Ben Kujak." Joanna surged to her feet and stood in front of him, hands planted on her hips. "Stop jumping over it. Say it out loud. What has her life been like?"

What had Evelyn's life been like? "She's had it hard. Been on the street." He looked up, smiling. "Did you know my mother was her mentor? I just found out today. I can hardly believe they were both in Memphis, and God used them to look out for each other."

"Really? That's great. I want to hear all about it later. But now, Ben. *Think*."

"I already said. She was homeless. She was dependent on places like Corinna's Cupboa—"

"Repeat that, please?"

Why had Joanna interrupted him? He stared at her, willing the pieces to slide into place like a jigsaw puzzle app set on auto. Instead, they fought like the wrong ends of two magnets. "She was depend—"

"Does anyone depend on Corinna's Cupboard?"

Ben frowned. "Well, yes. The pantry shelves are open five mornings a week, plus we serve meals to about forty people three nights a week."

"What would happen to them if the charity closed?"

He shook his head. "I'm lost. Why would that happen?"

"If you give it up for Evelyn. To keep peace."

"They wouldn't shut it down." An icy wave sloshed through him. "Why would they? It's in their daughter's name. Their memory of her."

"Are you sure, Ben? Absolutely, one-hundred percent certain from the bottom of your heart? Think very carefully before you answer."

Fran's tears. Max's stony gaze. Both had been in direct contrast with Darla and Maxwell's openness and smiles.

Ben rose slowly, eyes focused on Joanna's. "Okay, you might be making sense, but I still don't get it. Why would Evelyn jump to that conclusion?"

"Her entire life has primed her for it."

He raked his brain, hunting for clues. Any clues, no matter how tiny. "Maisie said she overheard her mom talking to you, and she sounded angry. It scared Maisie a little."

Joanna's eyebrows rose.

Ben wished she'd stop doing that. "What were you two arguing about?"

"About her quitting the greenhouse project."

What on earth? "But that doesn't even make sense. You just told me—"

"What matters most to Max Martinez?"

Chapter 22

*E*VELYN SAT IN DEMI'S DELIGHTS, twirling a cup of strong coffee on the polished table. She ought to be ashamed of making Nancy Poncetta come to the restaurant farthest from her accounting office, but she couldn't bring herself to face all the memories at The Jukebox or Sunrise.

The fifty-something church board member whisked in a few minutes later and hugged Demitria, the café's owner, before joining Evelyn. "Have you tried Demi's loukoumades? She's sending out a plate. I hardly ever come here because I just can't resist the things."

"No, I haven't been here before."

"Well, let me treat you. I certainly don't need an entire serving to myself." She leaned aside as the waitress slid a coffee cup in front of her. "I'm happy you called. I keep meaning to get in touch and see how you and your lovely girl are doing, but life is always busy. Why do today what you can put off until tomorrow, right?" She chuckled. "But it catches up with you."

"Mrs. Poncetta—"

"Nancy, please."

Evelyn nodded. "Nancy. This isn't a purely social visit. I'm in need of some guidance. Because you're a member of the church board, I thought you might be the best person to talk to."

"I'm honored. If it has to do with whether to say yes to that hunky young man who's been eyeing you, I say go for it. He seems like a solid catch. A believer with a heart for others."

Evelyn couldn't agree more. "That's not it, exactly."

The waitress set a plate covered with small golden balls dripping with honey on the table. "Is there anything else?"

"I believe that's everything for now, dearie." Nancy popped one into her mouth and nudged the plate to Evelyn before sighing rapturously. "This is what heaven will taste like. I'm certain. But do go on. If it isn't Ben, what can I help you with?"

"He's part of it, but it's more complex. You're an accountant, right?"

The woman nodded, but she was eyeing another loukoumade.

"Do you have a guess how much money it takes to run a charity like Corinna's Cupboard? Pay the lease on the building? Pay Ben's salary?"

"Hmm. Not offhand. I'd imagine it to be in the six-figure range somewhere The building isn't worth much, but I believe the Martinez family owns it."

Of course they did.

"The charity likely runs on donations. I know the family

has some fundraising drives from time to time. Local stores donate food, and the money helps fill the needs around that. I'd need to see statements before I'd hazard a more conclusive guess."

"This might seem like a dumb question, but..." Evelyn took a deep breath. "Is there any chance Grace Fellowship would be able to take it over?"

Nancy gave Evelyn a long, pointed look then tucked both hands on her lap as she leaned forward. "What do you know that I don't know?"

Evelyn rubbed her temples. "Hypothetically, is it possible?"

"Nobody asks these kinds of questions hypothetically." Nancy pursed her lips. "In theory, anything is possible. On the practical side, though... running a charity like that requires incessant fundraising or grant-writing. A church generally scrapes to meet the annual budget, so either the membership would need to be completely on board and dig into their wallets weekly to prove it, or someone would have to spend a considerable amount of time raising money. Someone with connections."

Someone like Max Martinez. Evelyn nodded slowly. It had been a desperate thought, but it had grabbed hold during the night, and she'd been unable to let it go. "Okay, thanks."

Nancy took another loukoumade and offered the plate to Evelyn.

She shook her head, staring at her coffee. Those little balls might as well be made of lead.

"Is there some concern about how the charity is currently being managed?"

"I'm sure everything is above board and running smoothly." The man wasn't sleazy, exactly. Just used to having his own way.

Evelyn sipped her coffee, avoiding the direct gaze of the woman across from her.

Nancy sighed. "You're not giving me much to go on here. Is it that you feel uncomfortable dating a man who works for a charity named for his deceased wife?"

"No." It had at first. "Corinna's been gone for five years. We talk about her. About his daughter, Zoey."

"Then who is it a problem for? Not Ben."

Evelyn shook her head, tears springing into her eyes and threatening to escape. After a night like last night, it was amazing her body had a chance to produce any more.

Nancy leaned closer. "Is it Max?"

Did Evelyn have to answer? Misery leaked out of her eyes as she met the older woman's gaze with a slight nod.

"That rat."

Evelyn did her best to even out her voice. "Accepting the fresh produce doesn't fit into the way he runs things. He... he asked me if I had the means to pay Ben's salary."

"Does he know who you are? Your relationship to Ben, I mean."

"He hinted. He didn't say it." Evelyn's chin quaked as she kept going. "Nancy, I can't come between Ben and the Martinezes. Not with the greenhouse. Not as a... as a person. The charity is too important to jeopardize. Too many people depend on it to keep them from hunger. I've been in their shoes, Nancy. If Max is the only one who can run it, and he insists on running it his way, then..." She spread her hands on the table. "Then he wins."

"Oh, dearie. We can't let that happen."

Evelyn fumbled in her messenger bag and handed over an envelope. "He wins."

"What's this?" Nancy gave her a sharp look as she slit the seal with a fingernail. She unfolded the paper, scanned it, folded it again, tucked it in the envelope, and slid it back across the table. "I refuse to accept your resignation."

"You can't refuse."

"But I do. When did this all go down with Max?"

"Yesterday."

"As a member of the board you answer to, I thank you for apprising us of the situation. What happens next is *not* this." She tapped the envelope. "What happens is a board meeting which will be spent in discussion and prayer. Only when we have had time to examine God's leading will this even be open for consideration. You're not in this alone, dearie."

But she always had been.

Nancy pressed more napkins into her hand as the floodgates opened.

"Again you do not have the attention span of a five-year-old." Felipe tossed the controller onto the coffee table. "I like to win, yes, but I would prefer to earn it by my expertise, not because you are staring out the window. There is nothing unusual there except an orange striped cat who is not even mocking you."

"What matters most to Max Martinez?"

Felipe blinked. "Come again?"

Ben poured more cola over the ice in his glass. "You heard me. You've met Corinna's father. What do you think of him?"

"Why does it matter?"

"Humor me."

"Okay." Felipe stared at Ben. "He is a successful real estate agent. I assume his wealth is important to him."

Ben nodded. "Agreed. But his family, too. He really loves Fran. Darla and Maxwell and their kids. He doted on Corinna and Zoey. He'd spend any amount of money to make any of them happy." He pointed across the yard at the paddock. "Case in point, a pony for a third birthday gift."

"So family trumps money."

That's where it got complicated because sometimes it seemed to, and sometimes it didn't. Max wouldn't be as happy with his family if they lived in row housing on the east side of Arcadia Valley as in their expansive Twin Falls home.

"You have said they are members of their church, so I assume he is a believer."

"I think so, yes. I mean, I have no reason to doubt it." Though Ben wasn't certain Max took that mindset into every real estate negotiation. The man had a bit of a reputation. And that reputation — his image in Twin Falls — mattered a great deal.

Ben surged to his feet. "That's it."

Felipe's eyebrows rose. "I may have missed something here."

"The thing that's most important to Max is what people think of him."

"That could be. My question is why that matters to you." Felipe grabbed a handful of chips. "And why this heavy thought kept you from killing aliens in the game."

Ben glanced at the time. Nine-thirty in Chicago wasn't too late to call Maxwell, was it? An hour later for Darla in Boston was definitely too late. "Excuse me." He grabbed his phone and spun through his contact list then jabbed the number. "Maxwell?"

Felipe wandered into the kitchen. A cupboard door opened and shut.

"Benjamin! How are you?" Loud music played in the background.

"Fine." Why was that the only socially acceptable answer? "Listen, I want to talk to you about something, if you have a minute. I need your advice."

The music quieted. "What's up, man?"

"Has your dad said anything more about the produce the Grace Greenhouse project is supplying?"

"Nooo."

"Or about Evelyn?"

"What's going on, Ben?"

"I wish I knew. I only have a few pieces, but I thought I'd ask you before I went over to their house and made a fool of myself."

"I doubt that's possible. What've you got?"

"Is there any reason to think your parents would close Corinna's Cupboard rather than keep me on as manager if I remarried?"

There was silence for a few seconds. "I can't imagine why they'd do that."

"I know your dad has told a lot of people how the charity was Corinna's thing, and how he hired me to run it in her memory. It made him feel good. I think he…" Ben took a deep breath. "I think he liked it when I was depressed and dependent on him. The vegetables threaten that dependence. Evelyn threatens it even more." It sounded so horrible out loud. "Please tell me I'm wrong."

Felipe stood in front of him, bag of chips in hand, eyebrows raised.

"Has he said anything?" asked Maxwell.

"Not to me. And Evelyn… well, she won't say exactly what she knows. But I think — and this is conjecture, mind you — I think he told her to back off and take her veggies with her."

Maxwell grunted. "If she loves you, why wouldn't she call his bluff?"

"Because she spent years homeless. Being responsible for the demise of a soup kitchen would be more than she could handle." The more he thought about it, the surer he was. "Is there anything else I need to know? And tell me — whose side would you take if it came down to it?"

"You need to ask that? Yours. You weren't responsible for Corinna's death or Zoey's. You may have been young, but you were a role model for me in my own marriage. Made me wish to be a better husband like you."

Whoa. Ben gave his head a shake to dislodge emotion. "You're kidding me."

"Not at all, Ben. Why should you spend the rest of your life alone when you have a woman who loves you? Just because my father has built a shrine for his daughter?"

"What about funding?"

"Leave that to me and Darla. I'll give her a call right now."

"It isn't too late?"

"No, they were headed out to a concert tonight. I'm betting they're just getting home. One thing, though. Give it to me straight. Ben, do you really want to keep running the charity? Is that where your heart is for the next few years at least? I'm not asking for a lifetime commitment, but if I'm going to bat for you, I need to know."

"That's a fair question." Without Evelyn — without Maisie — he might not have been so certain. And then there was his mom, whom he'd yet to talk to directly. Any guy could pound nails, but not everyone could change lives. "I'm sure."

"Keep Sunday evening free if you can. I'll see if we can Skype in. That work for you?"

"Tomorrow? I can't tell you what this means to me."

The man chuckled. "I've always wanted to go toe-to-toe with my father. Thanks for giving me a good reason."

Felipe stuck his thumbs through his belt loops and widened his stance as Ben laid the phone on the coffee table. "Are we visiting Max Martinez? Can I come in uniform?"

Ben eyed his friend, who looked every bit the police officer even in jeans and a T-shirt. "Who said anything about you coming along?"

"I did. You're my friend. You're not doing this alone."

Ben stared at him. The man was as strange as one of the aliens in the post-apocalyptic game.

Felipe's gaze fell. "No uniform? I will at least be packing heat. There is no question."

Chapter 23

"THIS IS A BAD IDEA." Evelyn sat in the backseat of Grady's Eos outside a mansion on the outskirts of Twin Falls. If Joanna and Grady ever had kids, they'd need a different car. This was way too scrunched.

"It's a good idea." Grady tapped his fingers on the steering wheel as another car pulled in behind them. Nancy Poncetta, Ernest Marshall, and Mr. Wattenberg were in that one.

Evelyn had been arguing for three hours, but no one listened. That didn't stop her from trying again. "You can't just march into someone's house and tell him he's an idiot. Even when he clearly is. It's going to backfire."

Joanna reached through the gap between the seats and patted Evelyn's arm. "It's not going to backfire. Just wait and see."

Waiting. That's what she was doing. Two cars full of relatively mature and sane adults parked outside a house.

Waiting for what? Christmas?

A third car pulled in behind Ernest's and the lights blinked off. Dusk had fallen. This was nuts. Kenia was home with Maisie and they were doing some Narnia craft project. Maisie was in seventh heaven.

Evelyn was going to puke.

Grady's phone beeped. He flicked it off and reached for the door handle. "Ready?"

"No. Don't make me face Max Martinez. I never want to see him again."

"I predict you'll see him many more times in your life, and that the two of you will find a respect for each other." Grady rounded the car and opened the passenger door.

Once Joanna had clambered out, Evelyn extricated herself from the back. "I'm returning to Arcadia Valley with Mr. Marshall, not in your sardine can."

Joanna linked arms with her. "You may if you must."

Two men walked up the sidewalk ahead of them. Evelyn dug in her heels. "You didn't tell me Ben would be here," she hissed.

"There are a lot of things we didn't tell you." Grady took her other arm.

"This is nuts. Really. It took one man to intimidate me, and we think it takes eight to make him even notice?"

Ben punched in a code at the door then entered. They all trouped in behind him, but he didn't stop to say anything. He and his friend disappeared down a broad stairwell.

This was a game an eleven-year-old would like. Evelyn gave one more longing look at the door, but she'd heard the tick as the lock reset.

"Follow me." Grady headed down, leaving Joanna and Evelyn to traverse together, the church board members behind them. "Shhh."

Like that was necessary. This was how Corinna had grown up? No wonder Ben's house was so nice. Different from cardboard in an alcove in an alley, that was for sure. At the bottom, Joanna pulled her aside as the others filed toward a brightly lit open doorway. A man whose voice Evelyn didn't recognize spoke.

"Sweetie?" Joanna whispered. "I know you're scared. But when everyone, including Mr. Wattenberg, thought it was a good idea — and you know what a pessimist he is — and we've all prayed so hard in the past couple of days, looking for direction... we've just got to trust, okay? Put your chin up."

Evelyn took a deep breath. Did she want Max to think she was a sniveling sheep? Did she want Ben to see her this way? No. She'd be like Reepicheep from Narnia, brave despite the odds. She straightened her shoulders and breathed her seven-thousandth prayer of the day. This was for more than her and Ben. It was for Rona. For Fred. For all the others.

Max's voice rose from the room ahead. "I do not recall inviting any of you into my home."

"C'mon." Joanna linked arms and they edged in beside Nancy Poncetta. The group ranged down the wall facing a giant screen.

"Welcome, friends." The fortyish man on the screen seemed to meet the gaze of everyone in the room. "I've invited them, Dad."

"Who's that?" whispered Evelyn as the screen divided to

show a woman of similar age in a book-lined study.

"Maxwell Martinez, Corinna's older brother, from Chicago. And their sister Darla in Boston."

Max whirled toward the screen. "I don't understand who these people are or why they are in my house."

"I haven't met them all myself yet. Please have a seat, Dad. Ben, would you go ahead and introduce your friends?"

"Thanks for the welcome, Maxwell. This is my good friend, Felipe Espinoza. He, uh, happens to be a member of the Arcadia Valley Police Department."

Felipe gave a sharp nod at the screen then at Max, hands flexing at his sides.

"These three folks are members of the church board at Grace Fellowship. They've been instrumental in helping with the operations for the greenhouses and gardens that supply produce for Corinna's Cupboard. Mrs. Poncetta, Mr. Marshall, and Mr. Wattenberg."

"Mr. Wattenberg! Good to see you." The woman on the screen leaned closer to her webcam. "You were my favorite calculus teacher ever."

The man dipped his head a little and smiled. "And you one of my most gifted students, Darla."

Evelyn blinked. Well, then.

"My good friend Grady Akers, whose grandfather entrusted the greenhouses and the property they stand on to Grace Fellowship, and his fiancée, Joanna, who also has worked hard on the project."

Then Ben stood in front of her, taking her breath away. His brown eyes softened as he wrapped his fingers around hers and stepped to her side. "And Evelyn Felton, the woman

I love, who coordinates an army of volunteers all the way through the production line."

Evelyn's heart soared as she smiled up at him and squeezed his hand. He was fighting for her. Only... who would win?

A middle-aged woman headed for the door.

"Mom, we need you to stay," said Maxwell firmly. "Please."

Corinna's mother scanned Evelyn with teary eyes before turning back to the curved sofa she'd been sitting on. Max sat beside her and took her hand in his.

"Okay, I'm going to call this meeting to order the way we normally do. Darla, are you ready to take minutes?"

"Yes." She smiled at the webcam.

"Dad, will you open in prayer?"

Max started visibly. "Me?"

"Yes. That's what you usually do."

"But..."

"Go ahead." Maxwell closed his eyes, clasping his hands in front of his face.

"Uh. Our heavenly Father, we thank You for Your many gifts and, uh, ask for Your wisdom. Amen."

"Amen. Thanks, Dad." Maxwell leaned into his webcam. "Most of you know why we're gathered tonight. There are two main items on our agenda. The first is the donation of garden-grown produce to the charity which bears my sister's name. I can't thank all of you enough for the hard work and vision it's taken to accomplish so much in such a short time. My family and I would like to thank you from the bottom of our hearts."

Darla nodded. "Our younger sister was so full of vitality. I know she'd be thrilled at the new direction the foundation has taken."

"How are plans coming for the next growing season?" Maxwell asked. "Is there anything you need that we can raise funds for? Because we've been buying less food, it seems there might be something else we can help with?"

"Thanks for that generous offer. I'll give it some thought and let you know," Ben replied then nudged Evelyn, tweaking his chin toward Max. The man sat staring straight ahead with a stoic expression and a twitching jaw.

"Please do. Darla, was there anything you wanted to add about this agenda item?"

"No, I think that covers it."

"Dad? Mom?"

The elder Martinezes remained silent.

"All right, we'll move on to the second item. Ben, you've been the hands and feet for the charity for five years now. I want you to know you make me very proud. It was an honor to have you as a brother, and just as much to work with you on this project as a tribute to my late sister."

Evelyn clutched Ben's hand. Why would he leave? But he couldn't. He really couldn't. Even if they kept operating the greenhouse, it wouldn't be the same without him there. Her life wouldn't be the same. She needed him as much as the charity did.

Maybe more.

Someone else could do a good job. Probably. But there was no one else for her. Just Ben. She stretched to whisper in his ear. "Whatever happens, I love you."

The brilliant smile he bestowed on her chased the last of the doubts away.

"I agree, Maxwell." Darla's voice rang through the room. "I can't imagine anyone doing a better job. So the question is, do you want to keep at it, Ben? Or would you prefer the foundation to look for someone else to run the day-to-day operations?"

Ben took a step forward, tugging Evelyn along with him. "A few weeks ago, I wouldn't have been so sure." He slipped one arm around her and kissed her hair. "But this woman here has reminded me of why it's so important. You know Corinna wanted to find my mother. I spoke to Mom today for the first time in fourteen years. While I won't pretend there aren't things I wish she would've done differently, I can't blame her any longer for abandoning me. She mentors homeless women in Memphis, because she was one. She understands." He glanced down at Evelyn.

"She was my mentor." Evelyn cleared her throat. "I didn't know she was Ben's mom until a week or so ago. She's wonderful." She beamed up at Ben. "I can't wait until you meet each other in person again."

Ben turned back to the screen. "To answer your question, Darla. With Evelyn at my side and my mom's example to guide me, I can't think of a better, more meaningful job than the one I've been doing. I'd be honored to continue on with Corinna's Cupboard indefinitely."

"Dad? Anything you'd like to add to the conversation?"

Max and Fran exchanged glances. Max shook his head. "No, if this is the direction you think is best for the charity, then go ahead."

He sounded so defeated, Evelyn almost felt sorry for him. Almost, until she remembered when the shoe had been on the other foot last Thursday. When he'd been in command, ruining not only her life but her work. Hers and Ben's both.

"Mom?"

Fran shook her head as she stared down at Max's hand grasped between both of hers.

"That's excellent, then. Darla, have you got everything recorded?"

"I do."

"And whom should I call if I have any questions about the needs at the greenhouse?" Maxwell went on. "Would that be you, Evelyn?"

She blinked. She'd tried to resign, but Nancy hadn't let her. She gave a short nod. "Yes, that's me."

"One more thing, off the record, since it's not the official business of Corinna's Cupboard..." Darla's voice trailed off.

"Go ahead, sis." Max nodded with a smug grin.

"We know there's nothing official yet." Darla's finger wagged back and forth. "But if Ben gets brave and pops the question, we want you to know you're very welcome in this family, Evelyn. He'll always be our little brother, and we care a lot about him."

Ben's hand on her waist tightened even as he pointed at the webcam. "While I thank you for your kind words and support, that's enough out of both of you."

Chuckles came from in front and behind. Not, however, from the couple seated on the curved leather sofa.

"It's late here in Boston." Darla's fingers flickered a goodbye. "I look forward to seeing you all someday soon."

"Good night." Maxwell waved. "Call me soon, Ben." The screen blanked.

"We're heading out now," whispered Joanna. "Sure you don't want to come with us?"

Evelyn shook her head. "I'll find a ride home when I'm ready." She stepped out of Ben's embrace and approached the sofa where Nancy Poncetta had taken a seat beside Fran Martinez. Ernest Marshall crouched in front of Max.

If they could extend graciousness, so could she.

Chapter 24

"IS THERE ANYTHING she can't do well?" Ben's stepdad leaned against the railing beside him one Saturday in October.

"I know, right?"

Evelyn had coordinated the town's most successful Harvest Festival ever. Even now the parade ambled down Main Street toward the fair grounds. Ben chuckled as a float decorated like a giant loaf of bread rolled by, the Baxter brothers waving at the crowd. A shiny pickup was next, with local sports hero Alex Quintana waving a bat while kids in team uniforms handed baseball-shaped candy to onlookers. The Friends of the Library had decorated a float with giant children's classics made out of — what? Wood? Cardboard? Ben couldn't tell. Several horses trotted next, two riders carrying a banner for Bigby Farm between them.

A float covered in kennels rolled by with Maisie and Kaleena running alongside it, offering dog treats to any bystander who'd take one. Riley waved and made a megaphone with her hands. "I've got your puppy right here!" she yelled at Ben.

He shook his head and grinned. There'd be no shortage of animals around his place. Not since Maisie had hooked up with Riley.

The parade trundled on, and soon the high school band marched past as the finale.

"What's next?" George asked as the drums faded.

"Picnic at the park. Mom and Evelyn should be there soon."

"I want you to know I'm proud of you, Ben. So's your mom."

He'd been hearing that a lot lately. More than ever in his life. But what had he done this time? He raised his eyebrows.

"For going to see your father."

"He was drunk. Both times."

"I know, but you went. We'll keep praying for him."

This man amazed Ben. Praying for his wife's ex? George had a true pastor's heart. "It's not going to be easy to stay in his life. Not for me or my sister."

"It's worth it. God never gives up on us. He just keeps offering His love and forgiveness until our time on earth is done. How can we give up when God won't?"

Ben grinned at his stepdad. "You may have to keep reminding me. Evelyn, too. She hasn't heard back from her parents yet, but at least she tried to reach out."

George nodded. "I'm glad she's found peace with it the way things are. Maybe, in time, they'll respond."

Evelyn and his mom strolled around the corner by Sunrise Café. His mouth dried. Evelyn had never looked more beautiful. She wore the lacy green top he loved so much over a pair of skinny jeans and a pair of low heels. But it wasn't her clothes. It was the radiance on her face.

So much had changed in the few short weeks since that night in the Martinez media room. Max and Fran had even taken them out to dinner to L'Aubergine one night. Fran had decided she liked Evelyn, no doubt with Darla's encouragement. Max was starting to come around.

Evelyn leaned against the railing beside him. "Hi."

Ben wrapped an arm around her waist and kissed her hair. "Hi, yourself. Ready for the picnic? Then I'm planning on dancing the night away with you and the Boys from Boise."

She chuckled. "That sounds fun."

"Your mother and I are too old for that kind of thing," George teased.

"Just the right age for having a sleepover with a grand... I mean gorgeous girl." Mom's eyes twinkled at the near slip. "Maisie's grown so much since Memphis. I can hardly believe it."

"Believe it." Evelyn rolled her eyes. "Eleven going on eighteen."

They strolled the few blocks to the park, where crowds funneled into lines to offer their picnic tickets. By the time they got to the food, Maisie had joined them, giddy from the excitement of the parade. As soon as they'd found a spot to spread their picnic, Maisie dashed away again.

Evelyn frowned as she settled onto the quilt. "Where's she off to this time? That child."

Ben watched Maisie returning, clutching a white short-haired puppy to her chest. Hopefully she had a very good grip on the green harness around the pup's chest.

"Maisie! Not now. Seriously. We're eating."

Maisie knelt beside Evelyn. "But look at him. Isn't he the sweetest thing ever?" The puppy dashed his tongue at Maisie's nose, and she giggled. "What do you think we should call him?"

Evelyn looked up at Ben with pleading eyes.

He wasn't falling for that one. He crouched beside Maisie and rubbed the puppy's head. "He is kind of cute."

From the corner of his eye, he saw Mom slide Evelyn's plate out of the way. "What is with the two of you? This isn't the time or the place." Evelyn gently nudged the puppy away.

"Just pet him, Mom." Maisie grabbed Evelyn's hand and brushed it over the pup's head. "Like this."

With another beseeching look at Ben, Evelyn stroked the animal. "Satisfied?"

"He's even got a really pretty collar, Mom. Did you see?"

Ben saw. Riley had done as he asked, threading the diamond solitaire on the harness, where it caught the late afternoon sun. Even now, Riley hovered behind them.

Evelyn's hand froze in mid-air then swung to clasp her mouth.

His cue. Maisie grinned from ear to ear while he unbuckled the contraption and carefully removed the ring. He'd picked it up at Facets on Main over a week ago, planning for this moment. Now he held it out to his beloved. "Evelyn, I love you. Will you marry me?"

She held out her left hand as he slipped the ring in its rightful place then raised shining eyes to his. "Yes, please!"

Ben pulled her to standing and wrapped both arms around her, twirling her around and kissing her. Not caring who witnessed. Hoping the whole town did.

It seemed they might've for the applause that enclosed them when he finally drew back.

Maisie's arms came around them both, and they included her in their circle. "So, um, when's the wedding? Because Riley said my puppy is old enough to come home with us in a couple of weeks. We can't have him in the apartment, and it's not fair to Ben to have to look after him for me."

"*Your* puppy?" Evelyn flicked a finger at Maisie's chin. "I thought Sprout here came with the ring and was part of my engagement gift. Doesn't that make him *my* puppy?"

Maisie looked from one adult to the other and bit her lip.

Ben could just see the gears grinding.

"But you don't even want a dog."

"Who said?"

Ben couldn't hold back the laughter anymore at the bemused expression on Maisie's face. Suddenly the girl's eyes brightened and she ducked out of their circle. "Riley! That means I still get my own puppy!"

Ben closed the gap and kissed Evelyn once again to the sound of laughter and cheering. There'd never be a dull moment in his life from here on in, but he was up for it.

Although Maisie didn't have a bad idea. Why wait?

Dear Reader

Do you share my passion for locally grown real food? No, I'm not as fanatical or fixated as many of the characters I write about, but gardening, cooking, and food processing comprise a large part of my non-writing life.

Whether you're new to the concept or a long-time advocate, I invite you to my website and blog at www.valeriecomer.com to explore God's thoughts on the junction of food and faith.

Please sign up for my monthly newsletter while you're there! My gift to all subscribers is *Peppermint Kisses*, a short story set in the Farm Fresh Romance series. Joining my list is the best way to keep tabs on my food/farm life as well as contests, cover reveals, deals, and news about upcoming books. I welcome you!

Enjoy this Book?

Please leave a review at any online retailer or reader site. Letting other readers know what you think about *Sprouts of Love: An Arcadia Valley Romance* helps them make a decision and means a lot to me. Thank you!

If you haven't read any of my other books, may I suggest the six-book Farm Fresh Romances? The first story is *Raspberries and Vinegar*.

Keep reading for the first chapter of *The Thought of Romance* by Danica Favorite, the next book in the multi-author Arcadia Valley Romance series.

.

The Thought

of Romance

— an Arcadia Valley Romance —

DANICA FAVORITE

Chapter One

Medical equipment. Gizmos and gadgets that belonged in a hospital, not a person's home.

Andrew Bigby pushed past the miscellaneous items stacked along the hallway by the back door. He took a deep breath as he walked further into the room. His grandmother was not that sick. In fact, when he got into the living room, there sat Gram in her favorite chair, sipping a cup of tea.

He bent and kissed her on top of her head. "What's all this stuff, Gram?"

Gram set her cup of tea on the rickety round table his great uncle such and such had made and looked up at him with a resigned expression on her face.

"That stupid caseworker Matilda Talcott. The nurse told her I wasn't doing what I'm supposed to be doing for therapy.

So now they've got some other nurse who's going to come in and take care of me. They think I need all this junk."

A couple months ago, Gram's children, a.k.a. Andrew's parents, aunts and uncles, decided to try to take over the family farm after Gram broke her leg in a riding accident. While their initial bid was not successful, they had succeeded in getting Gram assigned a caseworker. The caseworker was supposed to make sure that Andrew, his sister Allie, and his cousin Caroline were not abusing Gram, or exercising undue influence over her to gain control over her finances.

Andrew shook his head. What a joke. Only the not funny kind. Just a ridiculous waste of everyone's time. This wasn't about concern for Gram's care, but the rest of his family being angry at not getting their fair share of Gram's farm. Though the caseworker agreed that none of them were abusing Gram, nor taking advantage of her in any way, she kept butting in when it came to Gram's medical care. Apparently the way Andrew and his family took care of Gram, as in, treating her like a grown woman capable of making her own decisions, wasn't what the caseworker wanted. Gram didn't like modern medicine, and that was just fine by Andrew. Unfortunately the caseworker didn't agree.

Gram pointed at the other side of the room, where Andrew saw a petite woman who barely looked like she could lift a feed sack, let alone do any of the stuff Gram needed, sat.

"Hi," she said. "I'm Layla Avila."

"I assume you're the new nurse. I'm Andrew Bigby." This was the third nurse the caseworker had sent to their home to take care of Gram. Most of them got frustrated with

Gram's eccentricities and quit. He wasn't going to bother getting to know this one either. After all, she'd be gone just as quickly as she'd arrived.

He'd admit she was kind of cute, though, if a man were to be interested in dating. Andrew had given up on admiring a pretty girl a long time ago. Still, there was something about that long, silky hair and dark eyes…

No. Focus. Andrew took a deep breath and tried to smile at her. "What's with all the equipment?"

Layla folded her arms across her chest. "I'm afraid that's privileged information. HIPAA laws and all that."

So she was one of those. Fighting the urge to roll his eyes, Andrew turned to Gram.

"Would you like to do the honors, or shall I?"

Gram grinned. They'd had this conversation a time or two, and by now, a person would think that someone would have noted it in her records.

"We speak freely in this house. All the lawyer documents have been signed. I don't keep secrets from my grandchildren. Now, my blood-sucking children, well, that's another story."

This time, Andrew didn't bother hiding the groan. "I thought we were working on being nice, Gram. Remember your blood pressure."

"I am thinking of my blood pressure," Gram said. "Keeping it all in only makes it worse. I don't know how Edward and I raised such a bunch of greedy ingrates. Except for Adam, of course, may he rest in peace."

Andrew came alongside Gram and put his hand on her shoulder, squeezing it. Gram had been mentioning her late son more often lately, and he wondered if being forced to slow down was making her more aware of her losses. Andrew liked to keep busy for the same reason — keeping the pain of his own unbearable loss at a dull ache.

He'd only met his Uncle Adam a few times before Adam was killed in an accident. Since Andrew had only been a child, he didn't remember his uncle, except that he'd made Andrew laugh, and since Adam's death, nothing in the family had been the same.

Some people thought Gram was crazy, and maybe she was a little bit. But grief did funny things to people, and while Andrew didn't remember a lot about how Gram was before Adam's death, he knew firsthand how the death of a loved one changed a person. Poor Gram had lost a husband and a son. He'd only lost half that much, and some days, Andrew felt like the struggle to breathe was almost not worth the effort. He hadn't even gotten the chance to walk down the aisle with Mykel. She'd died too soon. If this was the grief he felt having been robbed of a life with her, how much more so did Gram feel her losses? No, he wouldn't judge her like so many did.

Instead, he gave her another squeeze. "Let's do what we can to keep you around for a while longer, all right?"

Gram smiled up at him with watery eyes. "Only the Good Lord knows how long we'll be on this earth, but I reckon I have so many questions to ask Him, that He's going to take His time calling me home. No one likes listening to an annoying old lady."

"You're not annoying, Gram." Andrew gave her another pat, then sat in one of the nearby chairs. He turned his attention to Layla. "Now that we've gotten that out of the way, why don't you explain to me what's going on? You can start with all the medical equipment in the house. Gram doesn't need all that garbage."

Layla looked at him in the same indulgent way a person looks at a child. "Your grandmother's rehab hasn't been going so well. She's been missing her appointments. She's also starting to develop some complications from not listening to her doctors."

Andrew turned to his grandmother. "That true, Gram?"

"They want me to do yoga." The indignation on Gram's face made Andrew want to laugh. However, he knew from experience that if he did laugh, it would only make her angrier.

"Yoga, huh?"

"Do I look like a pretzel to you?"

Andrew just smiled at his grandmother. "Nope. But Gram, you've got to go to rehab. That leg of yours needs some extra care so that it's strong enough for you to come out and help us in the garden. We're going to need your help with all those extra cucumbers you wanted planted for that new pickle recipe you're dying to try."

Gram frowned. "Mona already tried it. They're disgusting."

With a smile, Layla came towards them. "My abuela makes great pickles. I can ask her if she'd be willing to share the recipe."

Gram's face twisted into a scowl, and Andrew already knew what was coming. Why such a nice offer would set her off, he didn't know, but Layla would be running for the hills when it was over.

"I don't know any Abuelas. If I don't know them, then they must not be much of a cook. I know every good cook in Arcadia Valley."

Leaning in to Gram, Andrew said softly, "I believe abuela means grandmother in Spanish."

"Well, I don't know Spanish." Gram crossed her arms and stared at Layla. "I wouldn't be able to read the recipe."

"My abuela is fluent in English. We use Spanish words and endearments as a way of preserving our heritage." Layla spoke softly as she approached Gram.

"How about I bring you some of her pickles next time I come? Abuela says there isn't a food that can't be pickled, so I'll bring some regular pickles as well as one of her interesting varieties. I'm told you have rather unique food choices."

Andrew had to give Layla some credit. She was enough of an optimist to believe that she'd be coming back. He respected that. Even though he'd pretty much given up on hanging on to any optimism of his own long ago.

Layla was doing her best not to lose her temper with the cranky old woman in front of her. She'd been told that Enid Bigby was a nasty woman with a tongue as sharp as a razor. They'd specifically asked Layla to take the case because they knew Layla was good with difficult patients. As far as she could tell, the difficulty wasn't going to be with Enid, but with getting her grandchildren to stop coddling her. Already she could see the apologies on Andrew's lips for his grandmother's behavior.

"How do I know it's not poison? Does she put gluten in it? Does she know any of my children, who are trying to kill me?"

One of Enid's previous nurses had put in her notes that the old woman was paranoid about a number of strange things. Clearly she hadn't been exaggerating. Yet as Layla looked at the old woman's eyes, she could see genuine fear that she thought someone was trying to hurt her.

"Why do you think your children are trying to kill you?" Layla asked pleasantly, hoping to defuse the situation.

Enid glared at her. "Because they hate me. And they hate the farm. They want to destroy everything we've worked for."

"I'm sure that's not true." She looked over at Andrew, who shook his head.

"You'd think," he said. "But no. I've heard every single one of them say they hate their mother. And they also hate the farm. I don't think they're trying to kill Gram, but they have been trying to put her in a home for years."

"Which will kill me," Enid wailed, pounding the floor with her cane.

Andrew let out a long sigh. "I told you. No one is putting you in a home. Me, Allie, and Caroline have all promised you that. We'll do whatever it takes to keep you right here where you belong."

And there it was. The one thing Layla needed to do her job. She couldn't help but smile as she crossed the last few steps to Enid.

"Then we should have no problem. As long as you do everything I say, you get to stay right here. But if you continue to be noncompliant with your treatment, I'll have no choice but to recommend to Ms. Talcott that you be admitted for inpatient care."

Her words, however, did not have the desired effect. Enid smiled as she leaned back against her chair. "You can recommend, but you can't force me. I know my rights. And I have my lawyer on speed dial."

Andrew looked at Layla sympathetically. "Just so you know, she's not bluffing. We're not joking about how aggressively our family has been working to get Gram out of the way. She knows her rights inside and out, and now that Caroline is engaged to a lawyer, there's not a lot that gets by Gram."

The grandson meant well, as most of them did. But he obviously didn't understand that by helping, he was only making things worse. And yet, she couldn't help but admire how strongly he fought for the old woman. Most people didn't have that depth of loyalty.

"If the family is being as aggressive as you say, then why aren't you doing more to help your grandmother be in compliance with her medical care so that your family has no ammunition against her?"

"Because the doctors are all in on it!" Enid jumped up from her chair and immediately lost her balance, forcing her to sit back down.

Though many nurses would rush to her assistance, Layla could tell that Enid would only resent it, and her, even more as a result.

So instead, Layla kept her attention on the grandson. Weird to think of someone near her own age as someone's grandson, but she was someone's granddaughter, so it should have made sense. Except there was something different about the man before her. He seemed older, ancient, even, in the way he looked at her. But that was ridiculous, since Andrew Bigby was young, and, if she were honest, handsome. His sandy blond hair was tousled the way a model's might be, only Layla could tell that it was from the wind, and not hundreds of dollars of product. Though he was properly clothed, she could sense that he was muscular, not from hours in a gym, but hours on the farm. The weathered hands that tended to his grandmother were evidence of the hard work he did every day.

Exactly the kind of man she could bring home to her family and they would approve of. At least her father would. He'd done everything he could to shed his Mexican heritage, and resented the fact that Layla had wanted to reconnect with her mother's side of the family, who embraced being Mexican, rather than trying to dispose of it. Connecting with her Mexican side of the family had brought a missing piece back into her life.

Which was why Layla had no interest in dating at this point in her life. She already had too much on her plate with figuring out her new family dynamic — learning all the new people and customs. It was still strange to her to have cousins dropping by her apartment at all hours and dragging her out to family events. Besides, she couldn't date someone so closely connected to a patient.

Could she understand Andrew's dogged desire to keep

his grandmother happy? Absolutely. But keeping her happy and keeping her healthy were two different things.

Layla smiled at Andrew. Her cheeks would hurt tonight from so many forced smiles, but sometimes the job required it.

"Do you think your grandmother's doctors are in on the plot to harm your grandmother?"

He sat back in his chair. "Leave me out of it."

"Interesting." She shook her head at him. "You say you care about her and would do anything to keep her out of a home, but when I ask for your honest assessment of the situation, you refuse to give an opinion?"

Enid chortled. It figured she'd enjoy someone else being called out for a change.

"Fine." Andrew leaned forward again. "You want to know what I think? I think the doctors and the nurses have spent zero time figuring out what Gram wants, and how they can be partners in her healing. Instead, they're forcing their own agendas on her without even trying to see things from her perspective. Do I think that's coming from my relatives? No. I think it's a problem with the medical community in general. You play God with people's lives without considering the impact it has on those lives. So maybe, instead of forcing her to do a bunch of stuff she doesn't want to do, like yoga, you can figure out things she can do instead that will achieve the same objective."

Suddenly, Layla didn't feel so confident in her job anymore. As much as she hated to admit it, he had a point. She'd come in with her plan, and was prepared to implement it, knowing that Enid Bigby was a stubborn old woman who argued with everyone over everything. But was that the whole picture?

"All right then," Layla said, looking over at Enid. "We all know that you've got some health issues to deal with. But you're not taking your medicine, not doing your physical therapy, and making life difficult for everyone who tries to help you. So tell me how you think you're going to heal when you're literally doing none of things necessary for your healing."

Then she looked over at Andrew and gave him a small smile. Maybe he was right that people weren't looking at what his grandmother wanted. But since they all had the same goal of getting her well again, perhaps now he would see that she wasn't the enemy here.

Why she cared so much about what Andrew Bigby thought… Layla shook her head. It was just because he had so much power in Enid's life. But even as she offered that excuse, a tiny voice inside her called her a liar.

The Thought of Romance

is available through online retailers.
Find out more at
ArcadiaValleyRomance.com

Author Biography

Valerie Comer lives where food meets faith in her real life, her fiction, and on her blog and website. She and her husband of over 35 years farm, garden, and keep bees on a small farm in Western Canada, where they grow and preserve much of their own food.

Valerie has always been interested in real food from scratch, but her conviction has increased dramatically since God blessed her with four delightful granddaughters. In this world of rampant disease and pollution, she is compelled to do what she can to make these little girls' lives the best she can. She helps supply healthy food — local food, organic food, seasonal food — to grow strong bodies and minds.

Valerie is a *USA Today* bestselling author and a two-time Word Award winner. She writes engaging characters, strong communities, and deep faith into her green clean romances.

To find out more, visit her website at www.valeriecomer.com, where you can read her blog, explore her many links, and sign up for her email newsletter to download the free short story: *Peppermint Kisses: A (short) Farm Fresh Romance 2.5.* You can also use this QR code to access the newsletter sign-up.